THE ART OF FORGETTING

AHLEM MOSTEGHANEMI

Translated by RAPHAEL COHEN

دار بلومزبري - مؤسسة قطر للنشر
BLOOMSBURY
QATAR FOUNDATION
PUBLISHING

مؤسسة قطر
Qatar Foundation

First published in English in 2011 by
Bloomsbury Qatar Foundation Publishing
Qatar Foundation
Villa 3, Education City
PO Box 5825
Doha, Qatar
www.bqfp.qa

Originally published in Arabic as *Nessyane.com* 2009
by Dar al-Adab, Beirut

ISBN 978 9 9921 4264 6

Typeset in Adobe Garamond by RefineCatch Limited, Bungay, Suffolk
Printed and bound by Clays Ltd, St Ives plc

FSC
www.fsc.org
MIX
Paper from responsible sources
FSC® C018072

Love him as no woman has loved
and forget him like a man forgets

Dedication

I dedicate this book first to those who pirate my works. I know of no one who anticipates a new publication of mine as much as they do.

I owe them my popularity. If it weren't for them, the bookshops wouldn't be piled high with thousands of copies of my books – with the same cover as the original.

It gladdens me that all should find their means to a livelihood in this book: 'God makes me a forest and the people my hewers of wood.'

Glory to thieves, all of them. This is the age of the light-fingered, not the inky-fingered.

In addition, to *that* friend of mine
to her nobility in disdain, I offer up this book
to the women who have hitched themselves to waiting
and to the 'men among men' whose arrival changes destinies.

Communiqué No. 1

Fellow-thinkers that wish to join a new party that has no memory, no record of bank fraud, no blood-stained history, and no activist or fundamentalist slogans can sign up at www.nessyane.com.

Our only agenda is to confront the imperialism of memory and the past's emotional hostility towards us.

We cannot promise any ministerial portfolios. All we promise is to ease the burden of your disappointments.

We do not expect material support from anyone. Only your benevolent prayers will make us richer. People, wise up! Your only salvation, I swear, is forgetting. Let memory be your misery no more. Break away from your parties, your confessions, your nationalities and your livelihoods and join a party where all of us are equal before loss.

Readers of this book, please pass on the news.

Clarification to the men who steal into this book

O 'men among men' we shall implore God at length to once again fill this world with your species, and to help us forget the others!

This is not a feminist manifesto.

It is a women's inventory against masculinity and in defence of man, that captivator to whose charms we are proud to fall victim, because without him we would be neither feminine nor women.

Who says we give a fig about the virility on sale in pharmacies; or to the preening machismo that leaves its shirt open to expose chunky gold chains in the undergrowth and that adorns its fingers with flashy bejewelled rings? The manhood of expensive watches and luxury cigars that flaunts its elegance and its perfume, the model of its car and its brand of mobile phone, in order to hint at former conquests and seduce us to add our names to its list of victims.

What we desire from men is not for sale. Neither China nor Thailand can manufacture it and then flood the market with men's goods intended to fulfil the needs of Arab women.

Gallantry, pride, chivalry, the splendour of composure and nobility of character. The allure of piety, valour, and being true to one woman. The refusal to harm, and honouring the emotional pledge – when romantic generosity has a price. The willingness to defend the honour of the beloved, to the very last breath, continuing to stand by her even after separation. All these characteristics, I swear, are not commodities for sale. Simply listing them here prompts a smile and makes us conscious of how crippling our losses and how negligible what remains.

Where have men gone? This is the question on everybody's lips.

The disappearance of manhood has not only damaged women's dreams and futures, but the very order of Creation including the law of attraction between bodies.

Climate change is nothing but the Earth's protest that no men treasure her femininity. They have surrendered her, as they surrendered us to the 'invaders', and left us, and her, to destruction and wickedness.

Let women learn from Mother Earth. No one has been able to silence her or reach a truce with her. And she has not ceased to respond to their impertinence with hurricanes, whirlwinds, wild fires and floods. She knows with whom to be giving and against whom to overturn the table of Creation.

Let them convene all the conferences they wish against desertification, pollution, the ozone hole and climate change. The Earth is not concerned with what they say. She knows that true manhood does not say much. Its mere existence is enough to restore the order of Creation.

True manhood believes with an absolute and unshakeable conviction that it exists in this world to give, to build and to love, not to cause harm.

True manhood's most beautiful definition is epitomised by a French writer: 'A real man is not one who seduces more than one woman, but who seduces the same woman more than once.' Manhood has faith that suffering should not be the fate of those who love, that destruction is not the ultimate destination of every love, that not every woman can be replaced by another and that the struggles to win a woman's heart and to keep it for life are man's most significant and beautiful causes. And to this let those aspire, who have aspirations [Quran 26:83].

This book allows those men who steal into its pages to learn from the mistakes of other males on the basis of 'acquiring manners from the bad-mannered'.

They have to learn love from those with little love; to draw an example from the fates of liars, cheats, wise guys and ego-maniacs. Let them know that women have woken up from their age-old slumber.

To the real men, I apologise. I love their wicked intelligence. I am sure they will succeed in wooing women with their manly means, whose charms no woman will resist.

Men, to boost their self-confidence and for a laugh, will rope a woman into bringing them this book from which they are barred, so that they can chuckle away to themselves before they have even read it. For they know that women, like Arab peoples, will conspire against their own cause. They betray their own sex in allegiance to the ruler of their hearts: man.

That's why all women's achievements throughout history have been thanks to knights in shining armour who have tipped them off to the tricks of other men.

We will continue to dream of being close to those men, of being their mothers or daughters, wives or lovers, authors or muses.

These handsome men who inhabit our womanly dreams; who come to stay, to comfort and to give pleasure; to protect, defend, empathise and support; who walk away only to come back and who leave behind them no nightmares, wounds nor bitterness, only a searing longing for their captivating presence and an unspoken promise to return and seduce us like the first time.

How many times will we fall in love with them, with the very same giddiness and fervour, unconcerned with their grey hair and the trail of the years across their features.

Let them grow old confidently. Neither time, nor illness, nor death will remove them from our hearts: we, 'the women among women'.

How can a lifetime be long enough for the love of one man?

How can one man be replicated for all the men of the world?

How I got caught up in this book

I ENVY YOU THE GIFT OF WOOD, THE GIFT OF FORGETTING
O DOOR
YOU WILL LIVE AFTER ME

—The late poet Bassam Hajjar

The writer as guide to the emotions

WHAT USE HAS LITERATURE IF IT CANNOT TEACH US HOW TO LOVE?
—Camille Laurens

In his *Letters to a Young Poet*, Rilke offers those who wish to grasp the flame of poetry his advice on how to become a poet. He describes the Inferno that must be traversed before gaining the Paradise of a poem. More recently, the Peruvian novelist Mario Vargas Llosa (a good-looker as well as a good writer) published his *Letters to a Young Novelist*. Here he offers a lifeline to young novelists in their struggle to understand the complex alchemical forces of creativity, lost as it were, in the dark corridors of the soul.

The most recent surprise came in the form of one of the last poems Mahmoud Darwish wrote before he died, which he leaves as a testament to young poets. Here he offers his final teachings and makes a gift of his mistakes to those who will follow in his footsteps, saving them a lifetime of wrong turns.

How often have I wished I had the time and patience it would take to write *Letters to a Young Girl in Love*.

We are never taught how to love, how to avoid suffering, how to forget; how to recover from our addiction to the voice of the one we love; how to break the clock that counts the hours of love. Or how *not* to stay up all night, how *not* to wait, how to fight the tyranny of small things, and foil the conspiracy of memories and the silence of the phone.

How can we avoid wasting months, if not years, of our lives chasing after emotional delusions? How can we empathise with the one causing us pain without returning to his hell? Can we escape that hell without flinging ourselves back into the perils of first love? How can we emerge from every love affair alive and strong and, who knows, maybe even happy?

Will anyone tell us, while we're still crying over the loss of love, that one day we will laugh at what today makes us cry? There's much to regret in taking love as seriously as we do. For no one bothered to tell us that love is simply the most beautiful and painful of our illusions. It's really simple: the greater the love, the greater the disappointment. Love that is born through high expectations becomes too high for the lovers to reach. This is because it needs to transcend them in order to truly become love.

The writers who, across ages, cultures and languages, have acted as emotional guides for lovers lost in the alleyways and side-streets of love, are too many to mention. I have no such pretensions. I am merely a nurse with nothing more than a first-aid kit to staunch the bleeding of broken feminine hearts. Along with the cotton-wool, surgical spirit and bandages, I bring you a good deal of humour. Do you know of a better cure?

But it is for forgetting that I have saved my kisses.

'What you cannot avoid, kiss hello.' This book is no less than the seduction of forgetting. I have done no more here than blow it a kiss on every page. It's as though Ahmed Shawqi's 'inferno of kisses' applies to just those fervent kisses we plant on the lips of an inevitable destruction, a destruction that we desire more with every kiss.

I wrote this 'Guide to Forgetting' with a great deal of sarcasm. I want you to laugh; nothing deserves sadness. 'Is there any greater happiness than breaking up?' asks, or rather claims, Ghada al-Saman.

Ultimately, forgetting means turning over a page in the book of life. This might seem easy, but as long as you are unable to rip out the page, you'll keep coming across it in every chapter. It's not just your gaze which is arrested by it, but your whole life which seems to open at the same page over and over again As Malik Haddad comments in bitter irony, 'Yes, the page must be turned. Have you thought about its weight?'

The role of the author is to lighten the weight of that page as much as possible and to turn it for you. Allow me to try. Perhaps I can turn this page of yours for you. It's so much easier to turn other people's pages!

The four seasons of love

YOU WROTE ME
WITH A HAND THAT BLOOMED IN YOUR SPRINGTIME
WITH KISSES WHOSE SUMMER YOU WERE
WITH WITHERED LEAVES SCATTERED BY YOUR AUTUMN
WITH ICE ON WHOSE FIRE I WENT BAREFOOT TOWARDS YOU
—the Author

Some years ago I learnt that phrases from my books were being exchanged by lovers as text messages.

My delight at this news was matched only by my horror. What a responsibility to become the head of an order devoted to love, to acquire followers and adherents to my doctrine of the emotions, followers who, in my name, pass on words of whose truth I am not completely sure, and advice of whose consequences I have no knowledge. I have no fatwas* for them, no advice and no ordinances. Love knows not law nor doctrine.

However, I constantly find myself embroiled in the love stories of my readers. Even men have asked my help to solve their emotional problems. If I may digress; when *Memory in the Flesh* appeared fifteen years ago, every sort of lover flocked to me. I remember spending weeks on the phone bridging the sectarian divide between an army officer and the girl he loved. There was also the problem of a poet whose beloved had been secluded from him – totally like pre-Islamic times. She was prevented from leaving the house and using the phone,

* Islamic religious ruling.

and he was in the dark about her. I had to pretend to be someone else and find out how she was, after he had given me her family's phone number.

On one occasion, a man wrote to me from Jordan and asked me to phone his beloved on her birthday because she was refusing to answer his calls. He wanted me to tell her that he loved her and ask for forgiveness on his behalf for having wronged her (perhaps he had cheated on her). He said that I was his only way through to her, given how much she liked me, and how much influence I could have on her. He was lucky that his letter arrived on her birthday and that I went to the post office that very day to check my mailbox. I spent a while on the phone convincing her to stand by her love and give this lover another chance.

At one of Algeria's book fairs, a man came up to me and told me how delighted he was to see me. He said that he had visited the book fair on the off chance of bumping into me, because his beloved had asked him for a signed copy of *Bed Hopper* (which I had just published) as her wedding present. I inscribed a copy with a kiss for her and spoke to her on his phone. I promised them three days in a hotel of their choice in Algeria when they were married. It was clear they were university students who had nothing between them but a wealth of love. That was my most gracious promise of all, as an author caught up in the lives of her readers. However, they never called back. Perhaps they split up; perhaps she didn't like the book!

Over the course of a lifetime's writing, how many secrets have women unburdened to me, and how many stories about love have I accumulated. My notebooks are filled with thoughts and sayings on love which cannot all be contained in my novels. My initial intention had been to collect them in one book, but they became too many for a single volume. Once I started thinking about dividing them up by subject, they sorted themselves out according to the stages of love; that is, its four seasons:

the wondrous season of encounter
the jealous season of longing
the agonised season of separation
the splendid season of forgetting
—the Author

These form love's eternal quartet with their Spring, Summer, Autumn and storms of Winter. Only Ibrahim Nagy has been able to capture them in one poem, his masterpiece *The Ruins*. All the seasons of love overlap, and it is impossible to clearly demarcate the different emotions. It's no surprise that the season of forgetting spills into the season of separation, since one leads to the other. The amorous state is fluid and, over the lifetime of a loving relationship, feelings vary wildly and inconsistently. So the season of falling in love may well fuse with the season of jealousy and longing.

In this way, the project was transformed from one book into a series of four books about love. Perhaps women seem to take up the larger portion, in an effort to ease the emotional oppression they have endured as love's prime victims.

I was so enthused by the idea that I appropriated three months from a novel (that was nearly finished) to write this book. If I keep up this level of enthusiasm, I might be able in around a year to complete the series (say, God willing!).

Why did I choose forgetting as the first season, and not love?

Because it is upon forgetting that love lays the foundations of its new memory. Without forgetting, love cannot be reborn. It is also the season where men have the upper hand. They astonish us by their capacity to recover and move on. Whereas a woman may give up years of her life in order to forget a man who has robbed her of many years already.

As I wrote this book, women all around me were engaged in close combat with the past. Friends would ask my help to resolve their conflicts with their memories, as if I were a Blue Beret deployed by the UN to separate two warring parties.

To these anguished women, bleeding from the wounds of the past, it would not have been appropriate to offer a book on love. They had to complete their recovery first, to accept – like men – the notion of forgetting. As long as forgetting is open to all, women can leave the winter of love for its springtime.

A Japanese professor asked his students to define snow. One answered, 'It marks the beginning of Spring.' The student was a poet in the making. This definition sums up the idea that love blooms again out of the frost of endings and disappointments. That is, the melting snows of forgetting will, tomorrow, nourish the burgeoning pastures of a new love.

O sleepless one, sleep
remember the promise and wake
If the wound has not healed
then memory has wounded again
So learn to forget
And learn how to erase.
—Ibrahim Nagi

Let literature bear witness that I have delivered the message

LOVE, LIKE DEATH, IS A PROMISE UNBREAKABLE
AND UNFADING
—Mahmoud Darwish

The two greatest mysteries of life are, without a doubt, death and love.

Both are a strike of fate and have no explanation beyond destiny. Major creative works are therefore nurtured by the perplexing existential questions that surround them. No one knows why death strikes here rather than elsewhere, to take this person and not someone else, in this manner and not another. Nor do we know why we fall in love with a particular person. Why him? Why us? Why here? Why now?

Only those who have made it back, in one piece or wrecked, from a grand passion can recount its wonders, describe its magic and terrors and make us aware of its pitfalls and disasters, for the sake of God, or literature.

If literature does not assume the role of emotional compass in our lives, who will take it on? Who will prepare us for that great emotional adventure which will shake us to the core when we are not ready for it and whose aftershocks will reverberate through our destinies and our choices, even after love has ended and its earthquake subsided?

If seismic emotional tremors are our preordained destiny, just like earthquakes are preordained for Japan, let us learn from the Japanese then. Having discovered that they live in the middle of a seismic zone, they have got the better of earthquakes by being prepared for them.

A minor quake hits an Arab country: it totally wipes out a city and chokes life for a number of years. This is because the Arabs are inherently fatalistic. They let life take care of itself. In life, just as in love, they see no further than today. They are quite ready to die as victims of natural, or amorous, disasters because they have a genetic predisposition towards mindless self-sacrifice, for the sake of the nation and despotic ruler, for family, friends and the beloved.

The Japanese islands, on the other hand, stand firm every day in the face of the most powerful earthquakes. Each time, their skyscrapers emerge standing and their people stand up again. For them, repairing the damage takes a few days. Human losses are counted in the units of the Richter Scale, not its power: rarely do casualties exceed single figures – with the exception of March 2011's earthquake that triggered a tragically destructive tsunami.

Japan has worked wonders using its head: we have created all our disasters with our hearts.

What if we declared love to be a natural disaster on a par with hurricanes, earthquakes or seasonal wildfires! What if we tried to be prepared for the devastation by strengthening our heartstrings, made flaccid and naive by the love songs and Egyptian films we grew up with.

Just like Japanese buildings, built to sway with every tremor, we have to acquire the flexibility to deal with love's emergencies. We need to accommodate the emotional shocks that make the walls of the heart tremble and cause those things with which we have stocked our feelings to fall apart. Though we believed they were nailed fast to the walls of the heart forever.

With each love affair, we have to train our hearts to expect the possibility of separation. Before we adapt to the reality of separation, we have to adapt to the idea, for in the idea itself lies our misery.

What if we tried to prepare for love a little bit rationally? What if we strengthened our heart muscle with daily exercises to acquire patience towards the one we love? Resisted falling into memory's emotional traps where our future retribution lies? Entered love with a Teflon heart, that allows nothing of the past to stick to its surface. What if we learnt to leave love as we enter it, without wounds, without sorrow, armoured against emotional illusions. What if we learnt not to love in one burst, not to give ourselves completely, but to deal with this stranger not as a lover but as a coloniser of our hearts, bodies and senses? If we accepted the possibility that the lover's name, which now makes our senses sing, may become the name of an earthquake or hurricane threatening death and destruction?

O lovers, no matter how naive, good, or stupid you are, set the following words before your eyes: 'Woe to a friend who sees not the enemy in his friend.'

Let literature bear witness that I have delivered the message.

Love is a man not immediately
obtaining what he desires
—Alfred Capus

The suspicious reputation of forgetting

THINGS HAUNT YOU
OTHERS COLLAR YOUR MEMORY
THINGS THAT RUSH TO GREET YOU
OTHERS THAT TURN THEIR BACK
THINGS YOU'D LOVE TO KILL
BUT WHENEVER YOU ENCOUNTER THEM
THEY KNOCK YOU DOWN DEAD
—the Author

You write novels and poems about love. No one asks you whom you're writing about. You're not asked whether a person really needs to have lived every love they write about. (Were Nizar* alive, the question would have made him laugh. This Arab poet with fifty collections about love to his name only loved a few times in his life.) That is, the recollection of love has a more pronounced effect than love, which is why literature is nourished by memory and not the present.

But you say you are writing a book about forgetting, so the question becomes: Whom do you want to forget?

It's as though forgetting were more disreputable than loving. Love is happiness, whereas the effort to forget is an internal admission of defeat and dejection. These feelings arouse the curiosity of others more than news of your happiness.

The more significant revelation, however, is that those eager to

* Syrian poet Nizar Qabbani.

read 'Recipes for Forgetting' outnumber those interested in a book on love. The men and women around me want the same book. When I clarify for men that 'this isn't a book for you', they respond, 'It doesn't matter, we want it anyway'.

All those I suspected were happy gave themselves away in their enthusiasm to sign up to the Forgetting Party. Is emotional misery so great in the Arab world?

Nobody declares themselves openly. Behind their mask everybody hides some wound, disappointment, mortal blow. They are waiting to gain trust in you then lift the mask and confess: I couldn't forget!

Before these masses aspiring to forget and struggling for liberation from enslavement to amorous memory, I expect this book to surpass its emotional aims and achieve legitimate political aspirations. It has become essential to found an Arab political party for forgetting.

It will certainly be the largest nationwide party. The only condition for prospective members is the desire to get over emotional disappointments.

I wager that this party will find support from the Arab leaders, because they will anticipate that among all the things we forget will be how long some of them have been ruling us, how much of our wealth we have given them and their retinues, and how much of our blood is on their hands.

Let them believe that we will forget that!

We need to restore our emotional wellbeing as an Arab nation that has always suffered from failed love stories, among them stories of love for homelands that was not always reciprocated. Only then, when cured of our chronic emotional fragility, caused by a history packed with existential disappointments, will we be able to confront our rulers with the firmness of resolve appropriate to the battle. They would not have been able to coerce us were it not for the debilitating devastation deep within us. Failed love stories have robbed us of sleep and exhausted us. And the condition is worsening, due to the vulgar satellite channels that appeared to distract us from the bigger issues, marketing cheap love and pathetic emotions, to keep us, as we are, weeping for the tyrannical lover while forgetting other forms of tyranny!

> Our salvation lies in what is antagonistic
> to us, not what suits us
> —Ibrahim al-Koni

We demand forgetting

Do you believe we forget as much as we wish?
—Alfred de Musset

With apologies to dear Marwan Najjar, writer of the soap opera *We Demand Intimacy*, 'We Demand Forgetting', for this is the age of demands. Some people demand the application of international conventions, while others demand that the planet be saved from the dangers of global warming and some demand the lifting of the economic siege on Cuba, the banning of genetically modified foods, and putting an end to stem cell research. There are demands to change light-bulbs to save the future of the Earth, rationalise water consumption to preserve water resources and to protect the environment by not using plastic bags.

We women are ready to rationalise our consumption of credit cards, to not hold men accountable for wasting our water resources, to concede our share of oxygen (in spite of its scarcity in the Arab world). All of these in return for one demand: protection from the consequences of our idiotic attachment to the emotional junk of memory. We demand equal rights with men, in forgetting.

We swear the most binding oaths that after this we will make no further demands for equality: whether in wages, in employment, in inheritance, or even in driving a car.

The scientists occupied in stupid, pointless research must devote themselves to solving a problem that afflicts half the world's population. They must modify the genes of women's memory so that one day it will be possible for us to forget just like men, and to light our emotions with the latest energy-saving bulbs from the West, ones that consume less energy and nerves, and power our feelings with batteries that do not have an extra long life.

We demand better research into embryonic stem cells, and adult ones if they exist. Maybe we will discover the root of this affliction that condemns us to be faithful to memories that others have forgotten.

This is an appeal to scientists. We call upon them to find the cure that puts an end to the faithfulness to the past that is common among the female species. Or else to clone a new memory for us women like that of fish, whose time span varies between five and eight seconds at most.

Faithfulness is an incurable disease that these days only afflicts dogs, and the foolish among women!

How I got caught up in this book

IF LOVE HAS A PATRON SAINT, FORGETTING NEEDS A GODDESS. IT'S FOR CALAMITIES LIKE THESE THAT LITERATURE AND DIVINE PROVIDENCE WERE INVENTED

—the Author

When I said to *that* girlfriend of mine, 'Love him like no woman has loved, and forget him like a man forgets', she shouted, 'Oh my God, write it down!'

However, this idea isn't a slogan, but a stance for women to adopt through an intelligence born of previous stupidity.

One piece of advice followed another during our telephone conversations and my words of consolation to her gave birth to what would become a book. I had grown tired of individually rescuing women among my circle of friends and among my clan of readers from the grief of romantic disappointments. I considered that what I was saying to one woman was worth being shared with all women.

It started light-heartedly, for everyone volunteered to supply me with advice and the distillation of their wisdom.

I made my mistakes and those of the women around me a gift to *that* friend of mine. I researched these emotional fossils, which had accumulated over geological time to form a repository of female naivety, for the reasons why feminine disappointment conformed to a pattern and why examples of masculinity were always similar.

Then friends started demanding that I write what would be a

'Women's Guide to Forgetting'. In particular, there was my dear friend Dr. Hanadi Ribhi, director of Al-Erada for Consultancy and Psychological Studies in Dubai. She had called me five years before this to invite me to meet her patients whom she treated with my writings.

When she got to know me, she despaired of curing me of my follies.

Some time before, I had come across my novel *The Chaos of the Senses* on sale in a pharmacy on Al-Hamra Street in Beirut, alongside books on dieting, diabetes and heart-disease. Incredibly surprised, and much to the chemist's amazement, I purchased the book. I spent the evening possessed, reading it on the chance it would cure me of a certain psychological condition. It had been years since I wrote it.

Incidentally, selective reading is one of the latest psychotherapies. A book was even recently published in Paris that gives the titles of one hundred world novels categorised according to the needs of the reader's every psychological state.

However, reading a book in the inappropriate state of mind may cause psychological damage, just like taking the wrong medicine can be harmful. Which is why, in its second part, the book contraindicates the titles of the novels that one must avoid when in a specific frame of mind.

It remains to be said that the ideal treatment for all heartache is laughter and not taking memory seriously.

I wrote many of these recipes laughing wholeheartedly, like in those beautiful sessions by the fire at a great friend's house. (She has translated some of my works into English and was skilled at reading my feelings and sharing my sadness and delight until we no longer knew which of us was translating the other.) Sometimes a third friend would join us. She was truly an incredibly beautiful and cultivated woman and fiercely proud. Pride, by the way, is the common characteristic amongst my friends.

It's as though I've written this guide for myself as well. Perhaps I will reread it one day. Even though I hate to reread one of my books once it has been published (so I'm not tortured by the desire to rewrite), I bet that I will be the first to grab a copy when it comes out. Perhaps I will benefit even if only from one piece of advice I set down in it.

This is because I'm more in need of advice than my readers. But, as my mother would say, 'She left her husband's corpse laid out at home and went to offer her condolences elsewhere!'

And if one piece of advice was worth a camel, I would have given it to you for the grace of God. And just to spite some men, I would give you a whole caravan of camels.

It's as though this book has given me the illusion of wisdom!

I only ask for your prayers in return: for the good in this life and for mercy in the next one. I consider this book a charitable endowment and am confident it will be my most read and most pirated work, given what I expect in terms of the present and future flourishing of women's disappointments, and men's betrayals. This makes me happy and hurts me at the same time.

This 'guidebook' isn't one of my works that took three years or more to write. Some chapters of those works I wrote in tears as I defended those great and bankrupt national issues I once believed in.

Contrary to those novelistic works, this book whetted my appetite for laughter. So much so, I often had to suppress my tendency towards political or feminist humour so that it wouldn't be banned in most Arab countries. Even before its publication, this book changed the destiny of many women around me. Foremost among them, Hoda, the young woman who entered my life as a reader with a bouquet of roses, and left my house laden with the manuscript of this book. This was after she had volunteered to have it printed out of love for me and out of the desire to forget, which was sufficient reward for her. With every chapter that I sent her she reconsidered her choices made in the past.

Sometimes I felt I was writing this book for her sake and not for that other friend of mine, after a beautiful collusion was born between two women of different generations. It was as if she was the young girl in love that I needed to bestow upon the combined wisdom of women, just as Rilke and Llosa left their experience to young poets and writers.

Thanks to her delight at every crazy idea I talked about and her insistence, every day, that I provide her with what I had written, she gave me – I'm renowned for my laziness – the enthusiasm I needed to complete this book in three months. In so doing, I had to sacrifice the obsessive rereading of my manuscripts, which sometimes goes as far as my following the proofs into the press. I was suddenly careless about those who might find in this book an opportunity to attack me. If they see this as their road to fame, let them have it.

Forgetting is a feminist cause too significant for me to drop out of fear or superiority. I have never given up on a cause, which has made me the most read woman author in prisons, Israeli and Arab alike.

I was always the 'ninth' in every cell of eight prisoners, as I was told by a prisoner who called me one day on a phone smuggled into prison for essential calls – he had got my number after my appearance on the programme, *Khaleek bil Beit* (Staying In). Thus, being a friend of the imprisoned, it's no wonder that I wanted this book to be a gift to the women of love's Guantanamo Bay, languishing in memory's internment without trial, on charges known only to their jailers.

They have no liberator and advocate but me!

In particular, I wanted the book as a feminist challenge that I raise to myself, after my watchword became, 'Yes I can'. Winning the first battle is sufficient for a woman to become invincible.

Have you got the message?

The greatest discovery of all time is
that a person can change his future
by merely changing his attitude
—Oprah Winfrey

Telephone oblivion

Do not weep over the ruins of the encampment
or over the beloved once departed.
Sever the kinship that once joined you. Let them
be the same to you, one gone and one reunited

—From *Contrary Advice* by Abu Nawwas

Love has Valentine's Day. Lovers celebrate it and exchange cards and longings. But where is Forgetting Day, my lady? In a country where every day is a saint's day, among their 365 saints is there not one suitable for forgetting?

As long as separation remains the flipside of love, and failure the flipside of passion, why isn't there a Forgetting Day when the postmen go on strike, the phone lines go dead, the radio plays no romantic songs and we stop writing love poems.

Memory in the Flesh, 1993

My friend who is afraid of forgetting

TWO MONTHS WITHOUT US MEETING,
A CENTURY AND NINE SECONDS
—Yannis Ritsos

A friend of mine is going through the agony of a break up, with all the accompanying heartache and the delirium of unanswered questions that follow the lightening-fast fracture of desire.

She had confidence in the man of her life. She had a reservoir holding four-years of memories, and a blank diary that he promised they would fill together with beautiful shared plans until the last day of their life. She was the richest of us all; her man had filled the pockets of her heart with promises until she renounced everything apart from him. He was her master and commander. He was her weather report and compass to navigate the world. We, her friends, forgave her distance.

She was living a love that we all secretly envied her for. Then came the shock and her torment began. All of a sudden she was heading towards hell, and we could do nothing to help her.

The man who was for her the emblem of manliness, the very image of love, the man she had followed like a prophet, had forsaken her, and she was slowly dying before our eyes

Without warning or explanation he stopped calling her. His stated criminal intent was to murder her with silence.

For months she was attached by a drip to a telephone out of service, whose owner lived in another country.

She wasn't in the middle age of love: she was on the verge of a love legend. With femininc stupidity she donned the mantle of waiting and wanted no one but him to undo its buttons. In this case, any advice we gave her was useless. She was certain of his return.

Her proof came in the form of memories, text messages and promises. All she wanted was for someone to confirm her belief.

In the beginning, I indulged her delusions so as not to increase her pain. She would tell me her story like an epic romance full of amazingly beautiful details. Every lover needs to create their personal mythology, but in its details her story was in reality closer to the mythic.

When I visited her, she showed me the staggering quantity of phone cards that she had used to speak to him over the course of four years. Each card allowed for three hours of conversation. Laid out, end to end, the dozens of cards she had kept could have covered the distance from London to Beirut.

There was no doubt then. This man had really loved her.

She was happy at my conclusion, as though she needed my opinion to be certain she wasn't dreaming or fantasising. She regained her enthusiasm and switched her phone on to read me the messages from him going back to the early days:

'Your disappearing again means I'll die. Don't you dare disappear.'

'I need your voice to see.'

I asked her, 'Might he be dead, God forbid?'

She responded in embarrassment, 'No, his number rings.'

'Perhaps, evil away, he's gone blind?'

She answered, shamefaced, 'No, he's always on the Internet.'

She evaded my provocative comments, seeking refuge in other text messages. She read:

'I love you at every instant, even when I'm asleep.'

'I wake up from the deepest sleep every time you stop thinking about me.'

I asked her, 'How long has it been since he failed to wake up from his hibernation and call you?'

She mumbled, 'The last time he called was on the sixth of June at four in the afternoon.'

'Do you think he's memorised the date and time of the last time he spoke to you seven months ago!'

She was confused, 'I don't know.'

'If he calls you, ask him immediately, before any hellos or how are yous, when exactly you last spoke to each other. And what day in what month you last met. If he evades the question or gets the date wrong, hang up straight away and never answer his calls again for as long as you live.

'Love is not measured by the number of hours he spoke to you on phone cards, but in the months, weeks and days you spent waiting and counting the hours. Fidelity alone has an accurate sense of time: it forms the bone marrow of memory.'

As I expected, she took to defending him like a victim of abuse defends her abuser. 'But maybe he's suffering, too. Maybe he's as aware of time as I am; his feelings always matched mine. I won't forget the day I transited through Rome airport and called him from a phone booth because I didn't have a European SIM card. We talked for an hour and a half while I waited for my flight. It touched him that I had to stay on my feet for so long. At the end of the conversation I was shocked to hear that he, too, had been standing the whole time. Once he'd figured out that I was in agony talking to him standing up, he couldn't sit down. Do you think that a man who remains standing on his feet in his flat in London for an hour and a half because his girlfriend on the other end of the line in Rome has to remain standing has ordinary values? Imagine, when I praised his gallantry, he replied, "Real gallantry would've meant *not* telling you. I remained standing because I wanted to share your suffering, not to get credit for mine." This memory in particular has kept me going. My heart tells me that he's standing in the same flat with the same phone next to him, and that his heart is still tormented, missing a beat every morning at nine o'clock, because he knows that in some city of this world I'm in agony because of him. But this time, out of pride, he hasn't told me. Lovers may fall out and spend some time, long or short, apart. But they don't forget and they don't cheat. The ones that are like him anyway.'

I interrupted her zeal, 'If he hasn't betrayed you, he's betrayed your longing. That a man has been able to live seven months with you off his agenda means that you no longer count among his interests. You in turn have to get him out of your life, however beautiful your memories of him.'

She seemed reluctant and unwilling to believe that he had really forgotten her. Confronted with her sympathetic silence for him, I took a piece of paper and began to figure out for her what I personally deemed to be betrayal.

'My dear, this man fell asleep and woke up over the course of seven months, 210 times (excluding daytime naps). Not once did he feel – at night or in the morning, when he fell asleep or when he woke up – the need to hear your voice. Over this period of time, he ate three meals a day, that is 630 breakfasts, lunches and dinners. Yet not once did his soul hunger for you. He went through summer, autumn and winter, yet neither the heat of summer nor the chill of winter made him turn to you for help.'

'Not true!' She shouted. He replied to my festive greetings with this message: "I turn to no one but you to protect me against women and the cold."'

'How long has it been since you last met?'

'Since the twentieth of January.'

'Do you honestly believe that a man you haven't seen for eleven months has become a monk in your absence? That your memory alone protects him against other women and the London cold? Do you believe that since then he's been hanging around like a picture on the wall? That not one woman has passed through his life, not one woman has sat at his table, stretched out on his bed or left her voice on his phone? Or even just kept him company on the Internet through the restless mornings and sleepless nights of the freezing north?

'Sit and ask yourself this question: If I said to you that I had faith in the loyalty of a man who had refused to answer my calls for seven months and whom I hadn't seen for a year, wouldn't you think I was naïve?'

Her eyes became teary and she said, 'Do you think that jealousy alone could drive him to have flings with other women just to kill time in revenge?'

'He'll do that to kill the you inside him.'

'But why do that when no woman will love him as I did?'

'Exactly because you loved him like no woman has. He will try to destroy you with another woman, until nothing in you remains strong enough to love any man but him!'

It was as if this idea stunned her. A veil of tears passed over her eyes and she said nothing. A mixture of pride and stupidity made her refuse to believe the possibility of being betrayed by the one she loved. We measure the loyalty of those we love in accordance with our own loyalty.

Moreover, her admission that this epic romance had come to an end because they outdid each other to be hurtful was to admit that she had wasted four years of her life. That is forty-eight months, 1,460 days, 35,040 hours or 2,102,400 minutes for the sake of nothing.

Good God! More than two million minutes with not a single one left; not even a single word on the phone to bring love back to life.

What kind of love is this that sweeps you along like a flood when it arrives and leaves you thirsty in its wake? That does not spare you one drop of loyalty to the past, just to validate the waste of those precious years of a woman's life.

I left her a written inventory of her numerical losses on the Love

Exchange, in the hope she might learn not to invest in delusional schemes.

Four years in the life of a woman in her forties is an irredeemable wealth of time.

This friend of mine is representative of thousands of Arab women. They offer up years of their lives in sacrifice to a man who offers them nothing but promises. They envisage love as a pledge to a man not necessarily pledged to them, but rather a hostage to his moods, his preconceptions, his complexes and his personal ambitions.

A man, like a lizard, sheds his skin and his past without misgivings. Only a woman lives with a memory crammed full of junk. She remembers dates by heart. She hoards text messages as though they were title deeds and copies them into special ledgers along with their exact hour and minute and second. She does this so she can recall the time of passion and parade with it in front of love itself. It's as though she knew that one day she would only possess these details she had recorded as the proof that he really did pass through her life.

Such stupidity!

I shouted at her, 'This love is dwindling every day, as is your life. A lost love is better than a dysfunctional love. Come out of mourning for this man, and make up your mind to end this relationship. Whatever the price of ending it, it will never be more than the misery of staying like this, "in limbo, neither married nor divorced", as my mother would put it.

'Plus, if you don't sort this out, you should know that you'll lose me. I just don't have it in me anymore to accept a woman's passivity and her willingness to make worthless sacrifices.'

The next day she called me, not as usual, but at nine o'clock in the morning. I was still sleeping, for I stay up very late writing.

She said, 'I'm calling you to say I've acted on your advice. Last night I took the decision to forget him and I wanted you to know.'

'You couldn't have waited till later to break the news?'

She answered laughing, 'Actually, I still wake up at the same time that he used to call me at for years.'

'Until you break the biological clock of his love, this man will never leave you. It's as though you are calling me now to tell me the opposite of what you intend.'

She replied sheepishly, 'I confess. I haven't been able to find a cure for the nine o'clock call. Or more correctly the seven o'clock call London time.'

'As long as he's been cured, you can be too. Don't let the clock control you. You're not one of Pavlov's dogs. Break this habit with a new one. Speak to someone else.'

'There isn't anyone else in my life.'

'I don't believe that a woman like you has no one.'

'No. I swear.'

I sat on my bed and an idea struck me. I said, 'What do you think about me calling you every morning at nine o'clock?'

She shrieked like a child, 'Wow. That's a great idea. I don't believe you'll wake up early for my sake!'

'It isn't for your sake, it's for the sake of forgetting. Let's agree first, my phone call won't be the call of love. It'll be a call to forget. Every day I will tell you about what other men have done to other women. And day after day you will rebel against your heart until you loathe that man.'

'But I don't want to hate him. I just want to forget him.'

She fell silent as though she were before an unanticipated choice.

I said, 'Decide. Do you want me to call you at his time or not?'

Perhaps her need for the phone to finally ring at that time was greater than her need to hear me. Besides, she had hope that we might touch upon his memory. But I wouldn't be so foolish as to call her and, instead of helping her to forget, fall into the trap of her memories.

She answered, 'I'd be really happy if you called me. You know . . . I like this female conspiracy.'

I said jokingly, 'You don't know what I did twenty years ago in Paris to save my cleaner from the clutches of a man.'

She replied with a gasp, 'Tell me what you did!'

I said, 'You will hear that story later. Every day I will tell you a story, the difference between this and *1001 Nights* being that my stories will be told during the day, not at night, and that I do not intend them to save my head from Shahrayar but to eliminate the Shahrayar settled in your head!

'I will tell you, like Scheherazade's stories "with all the words time permits", about your life that is only allowed in the name of love.'

From that day on, every morning the 'call of forgetting' would ring in my friend's house at nine o'clock.

Every morning when I awake I say,
'I shall forget you today too.'
Every day
for days
I always remember
to forget you
—the Author

My lovelorn cleaner and the magic recipe

SAY FAREWELL TO PATIENCE; A LOVER HAS BADE YOU FAREWELL
REVEALING THE SECRETS THAT HE HAD PROMISED YOU
IF AFTER YOU MY NIGHT BE LONG, YET MANY I SPENT
COMPLAINING HOW SHORT THE NIGHT WITH YOU
—Wallada bint al-Mustakfi

In the second week of forgetting, to rescue my idiot of a friend from her destructive longing, I found nothing better than an old recipe for getting over a lover (I believe I am the patent holder). I invented it twenty years ago in Paris when I was confronted by a girl ready to kill herself because of a man's cruelty.

Necessity is the mother of invention, and the girl really needed emotional support if she was to survive. So I said, 'Let's try the recipe on her.' I'd also been trying out drafts of *Memory in the Flesh* on her when she finished the housework. I would ask her how she found the story and the dialogue. The poor girl would discuss with me as far as her education and my head permitted: it was clear that I was out of my mind. Nizar was absolutely correct in what he wrote about *Memory in the Flesh* when he said to the late Dr Suheil Idriss, 'Let her go crazy. Creative masterpieces are only written by the mad.'

Since Nizar condoned my madness, I no longer feel a sense of shame in being open about my follies.

She was a Moroccan girl who had failed the *baccalauréat*. She wasn't in the least bit attractive and had come to me with her rustic plaits and wild features. She was living with a relative and came every day to help for a few hours with the housework and childcare.

One day the girl fell in love with a Syrian man; I don't know where she had bumped into him. He had been a teacher in Syria and become a handyman in Paris. The man had a Levantine handsomeness that she boasted about. She carried his photograph wherever she went. The girl gradually lost her bearings, having fallen madly and jealously in love with him. The man, however, did not lose his mind. He was just having a good time, 'a man who fancied her', as the Lebanese put it.

I found myself caught up in her story. She would ask me to write love letters on her behalf (after she discovered my literary talent). The man discovered subsequently, when she showed him my magazine articles and picture, that she worked for an author and that the letters were more beautiful than their carrier. (Her story deserves a novel!)

One day he decided to dump her despite my efforts to make her beautiful, cutting her plaits and giving her my finest clothes. My mother was convinced that the girl was using black magic to keep me under her spell. How else could I have excused her from looking after my three children and devoted my time to serving her? I would reply that if she knew magic she would have bewitched the man in the first place. Her condition became so miserable and piteous that I put *Memory in the Flesh* to one side and busied myself in ghost-writing her love life.

Whenever she called him he hung up on her. If she knocked on his door, he threw her things in her face. Eventually, the idea of suicide began to take hold: her death would be vengeance against him or she would at least cause him some pain. She was Berber from the Moroccan Atlas and first love, for her, was true, proud and fierce, charged with an emotional cocktail ready to explode and wreak havoc.

I reached an agreement with her that she would call me whenever she felt the urge to call him, and I would slur him, curse him, and his father, and shout at her: 'How can you allow a handyman to do this to you? Who does he think he is hanging up on you? You earn more than he does. Your background is better than his. If he had any decency he wouldn't treat a woman like this. Besides, it's you who fed his ego by asking me to write letters the likes of which not even George Sand wrote to Chopin. No wonder he started to think he was Fahd Ballan.' (The late Syrian singer was a macho type in those days).

'Ignore him. Let him suffer and chase after you. Besides, the sales are on. Go to the shop where I buy my clothes next to the children's school and get yourself something beautiful. Then the next time he sees you he'll chew his fingers in regret for having left you.'

Of course it was more likely that the guy was busy 'chewing' his latest victim. But I would say anything to her that strengthened her resolve to stand firm and forget him.

Afterwards, when she would come to visit me in all her elegance and my mother happened to be present, my mother would carp at me all evening on her account. 'Have you ever seen a woman send her servant to the same shop where she buys her clothes. What will people say when she dresses like you!'

'We're in Paris, mother, no one cares what you wear. The poor girl was going to kill herself.'

'Kill herself?!' screamed my mother. 'You're the one who's killing yourself. Just hold on and see what this 'mentor' of yours is going to come up with next.'

'In the recesses of your soul/desirous of servants/it's likely you more and more the servant./Of whom? Of what?/So seek, seek.' So said Henri Michaux. But I had neither the wish nor the time for seeking.

My mother insisted that I was bewitched, being at the beck and call of my domestic help. As for my husband, he didn't believe all these phone calls were with the cleaner. She would call me from any phone booth she passed to tell me the latest developments in her story. I couldn't call her back as the mobile had yet to be invented. I spent the time her phone card permitted alternately cursing and sowing doubts. I now ask myself if I was in my right mind at the time. How could a woman with three children, the youngest two years old, add to her maternal duties the role of Mother Teresa?

Because I seem to be compelled to rescue those women who are illegal immigrants on the boats of love, lured by some man towards the promised land of passionate love, then forgotten out at sea.

I've spent my life rescuing moronic women from overwhelming love affairs. In this book I continue to do nothing less.

That's why I asked *that* girlfriend to call me whenever she was struck by a desire to call him. I would tell her things about men to cure her and make her forget their kind.

Men are slain by hate, women are slain by love
—Ovid

The painful awakening from amorous stupor

DON'T WAKE UP A WOMAN IN LOVE. LET HER DREAM,
SO THAT SHE DOES NOT WEEP WHEN SHE RETURNS
TO HER BITTER REALITY
—Mark Twain

Good morning. It's nine o'clock Forgetting Time.

Your hibernation is over, my dear.

Arise from under the rubble. Arise from your sadness, arise. Open the shutters of your life lest frost permeate and cling to your heart. You, who were once a gazelle, have become a polar bear dormant for seven months. What injection has anaesthetised you? A Crush? Romance? Ardour? Fervour? Infatuation? Abandon?

Do you know how many names love has? Ninety, each according to the intensity and madness of the passion. You will know from the length of your coma what level of passion you had reached when you fell into an eternal sleep on top of that fluffy cloud with your dreams for a pillow.

You didn't expect the cloud to burst and hurl you to the ground from the towering heights of illusion. For this reason you didn't take with you, like a parachutist, anything to ensure your safe landing. A sudden drop wasn't part of your plan. Now your heart keeps hearing the sound of things breaking inside you that will be so difficult to repair.

Don't let the image of destruction spoil your mood and cripple your ability to resist. 'If we fall seven times, we pick ourselves up eight', say the Japanese. Stand up. What awaits is better than what surrounds you. Buy your dreams a new pair of shoes and you'll find all paths to happiness open before you.

Your waiting is in vain.

Neither love nor forgetting can do anything for you now. There are no ships on the horizon, so just leave the harbour of waiting.

He will not return as long as you are waiting for him.

You will never win him until he's lost you. You will never keep him unless he's deprived of you.

There are men you can't win except by loss. When you've truly forgotten him, he'll remember you. Because we don't forget what we lose!

Remember! Each time the winner wins, he loses
—Henri Michaux

Don't seek emotional asylum in bed. It'll hand you over to the enemy

INDEED I LOVE SLEEPING AT STRANGE HOURS
PERCHANCE A RENDEZVOUS IN SLEEP
—Lubna's Qais

Good morning. It's me.

I've taken to waking up early because I have a date with you. You stay in bed because you have a date with him.

Bed isn't a safe place for a woman in search of forgetfulness. Don't seek emotional asylum in it. It will hand you over to your enemy, the lover, in the same way that Sudan handed Carlos 'the Jackall' over to France and in much the same way that the Arab regimes hand over every dissident who entrusts them with his life and seeks asylum.

Bed is an ambush that the heart, bleeding with desire and plagued by passion, sinks into. This is in the belief that, due to its great familiarity, it is a safe haven

Actually, the greatest danger comes from that familiarity. Within it, you are held hostage in yourself. The boundaries of your domain are you; you're restrained from every side by memories and grief. You are the prey of a memory that you think you can escape from to bed.

But memory will savage you in bed, because you are there not to forget the one you love but to bring him back, to be alone with him, to weep for him.

Even sleep will forsake you. According to the latest scientific research, one of the functions of sleep is to protect the memory. Sleep helps the brain to store everything one believes one has forgotten in the course of the day. Sleep becomes an opportunity for the brain to restore memories.

That's why some people wake up with their pillows soaked in tears. They have been crying in their sleep; the wound still wide awake. Sleep itself is no longer a chance to forget, so say the scientists. 'People are not real except at the moment they are alone in bed', according to the Swedish writer Anne-Marie Berglund.

The most perilous place for you is in bed. It stokes your sadness, revives your pains and tricks you into imagining that you will meet there the man that you no longer have hope of meeting in life. Which is why they call the bed a place to lie!

'With a fleeting glance, many memories stretch out on my bed', says Einaya Jabir.

Get out of bed as soon as you wake up. Tomorrow I hope to find you sipping a cup of coffee on the balcony of your dreams. Sit by yourself every morning contemplating nature rather than sitting in bed with your memories.

Have you ever seen a man stuck in bed in mourning for a woman?

Instead he uses going to bed as a means for forgetting. He turns for help to a woman to forget another. And therein lies the secret of his cure. Sex for him is a medicine that becomes easier to swallow after each romantic failure.

As long as you remain incapable of betrayal, the least you can do is get out of bed so it's not his pleasure ground. It's the grounds for your misery.

Sex is the consolation you have
when you can't have love
—Gabriel Garcia Marquez

You Fool. Life's waiting for you but you're waiting for him

WHEN I AWAKE YOU ARE MY FIRST THOUGHT
WHEN MY EYELIDS CLOSE YOU ARE MY LAST
—the Author

A forgetful morning to you . . .

Truthfully, aren't you better this morning? For months you've been sleeping with your back to your body which lies next to you. Over time you've become your body's neighbour, your life's neighbour, not its owner. You're living a life put on hold until his return.

Such is the Arab woman: she defers joy in the anticipation of happiness. Life exists for your sake, with its scents, its flowers, its seasons and its encounters.

Life is waiting for you, but you're waiting for him. Happiness longs for you, but you long for him. Love loves you, but you love him. Because he is your pain.

Like a cat hankering after someone to strangle it, you want him.

When disappointment becomes too much and the reserves of feminine patience, despite their depth, are exhausted, you must reconsider your relationship with pain. For pain is not a destiny, it's a choice.

A year's worth of pain is more than enough, and this is the average amount of a woman's wasted time needed to get over a man who has infected her with lovesickness. A minor emotional complaint takes less time. There is a kind of 'love' that women catch like flu in the wintertime of the heart.

That kind of 'love' was not destined to endure for more than one season, and it wasn't worth your time in the first place. In this case, mourning it shouldn't take more than a day. But when faced with the pain of a major separation you must consider the questions it raises. When a loved one dies, being faithful means that you keep him alive in your heart until you die. There are some who spend the rest of their lives forever faithful, in body and soul, to the one they have lost.

Equally, it's only fair not to keep in your heart for more than a day someone who has chosen to abandon you. You shouldn't grieve over someone like that for more than a few days at the very most. It's a form of stupidity to keep alive in your heart a man who doesn't care if you die from abandonment. Ask yourself whether you are certain that on the other side, there is an ardent lover stepping out of the mists of the past, to weep for you and be true to your absence.

Stop being an idiot, for God's sake!

Set your watch to the beat of your heart,
and you will see that life is but a moment
—Popular saying

Memory memory memory out out out!

I WATER THE FLOWERS IN YOUR ABSENCE
YET THEY REFUSE TO BLOOM
—Ghazi al-Quseibi

A rosy morning to you.

It makes me happy to see you start your day tending the plants in your garden, but beware of messing with the tree of memory, watering it at every opportunity with nostalgia and expectation, and then being amazed that forgetting does not bloom.

Forgetting does not flower in the first season. It needs two or three seasons to mature. In the beginning it gives you its thorns. Don't rush it and don't worry. Harvest time will come. Love's calendar does not follow the logic of the seasons.

Forgetting is neither beautiful nor quick. No one can make you a gift of it before it's due, or sell it to you before it blossoms. You must acquire it at the cost of your pain, insomnia and tears.

These are the only currency that feelings deal in when facing a significant loss.

Remember too that we only forget when we truly want to.

Be truthful in your insistence on forgetting.

Men succeed in forgetting quickly because they really want to (in order to start a new relationship), whereas women fail because they are actually scared of forgetting (for fear of embarking on a new experience). Following the logic of 'a memory in the hand is better than forgetfulness in the bush', women are afraid that, upon forgetting, the last bird they caught will fly off.

Whenever a woman loves, she expects life never to give her the gift of love again. Hence her obsession with the words 'for ever', with which the man reassures her until he flies off, for ever.

Women must get over their feminine fear of the unknown. Men are no less scared than us, nor more confident of what awaits them. They are simply more capable of being unfaithful and of breaking their promises. Forgetting is a path that leads to the threshold of a new love. Some women, however, when the path grows long, become used to it. They fail to come out of this state because they're immersed in the painful pleasure of forgetting. The agonising path to forgetfulness becomes so pleasurable that it distracts them from any new love. That is, there is a masochistic aspect to a woman's makeup that is not found in man, who is a sadist by nature.

Well and good. The days of 'Forget you, what are you saying/ Forget you, my my/That's ever so impossible/Never even dreamed of' are over.

Be honest, don't you find these words ridiculous when you read them devoid of Umm Kalthoum's voice, the beauty of which could convince us of anything?

We might have believed them and died for them. We might have gone out on mass feminist demonstrations to condemn forgetting as an aspect of imperialism. We might have accused forgetfulness of participation in the great conspiracy against the emotional future of the Arab nation. Only had we seen men chanting the slogan, as they do for their leaders, 'With our souls, with our blood, we will redeem you, faithfulness'.

But what happened instead was that for ages men have been demonstrating to us that forgetting is very doable. We only want to show them that they don't have a monopoly over it.

Someone has to wean you off your past. Cure you of your addiction to memories that eat away at your body and thin your dreams. Forgetfulness is the only calcium against the brittleness of a lover in the face of separation

—the Author

Keeping the cage door half open

IF YOU REALLY WANT SOMETHING, SET IT FREE AND LEAVE THE CAGE DOOR OPEN. IF IT COMES BACK, IT WAS ALWAYS YOURS. IF IT DOESN'T, IT WAS NEVER YOURS TO BEGIN WITH

—Popular saying

I started phoning her in the mornings of pain to save her from memory's whip.

Like giving love a sandwich instead of inviting it to dinner, I was aware that my words didn't completely satisfy her, but they did provide her daily sustenance of vitamin E for Endurance.

Day after day, she seemed to be getting over the past. Or perhaps she was trying to convince me of this. However, nothing tangible had really changed in her life. She rarely accepted invitations or attended events. She lived her mourning gracefully and alone, but with greater tranquillity.

I would shout at her in despair, 'Where will love come from if you don't open the door to it?' She would answer, 'But I've left the door open.'

Later on I realised we weren't talking about the same door. I was talking about the door of life: she meant the door of the cage!

You're leaving the cage door open in the hope of the bird returning. This means that you're shutting all other doors, without acknowledging it to anyone.

Putting off happiness at hand, for the sake of happiness in the bush.

Choosing to lose the present so as not to lose the potential of a dream.

You must, every day, not forget totally and not remember totally.

Not abandon, yet not return.

Not telephone him, even though his voice inside your head is still telling you in the words of the past that he will return.

Not enjoy yourself too much, or you'll be unworthy of your love story.

Don't let sadness give you away and make you an object of pity.

You must find the necessary distance between you and him in absence . . .

Between you and others . . .

Between you and the memories . . .

Between you and the possibility of someone trying to come to you through another door, not the cage door, to occupy his vacant place in your heart.

Not to betray one who may have betrayed you, and not to be hurt by your loyalty to him.

To be faithful to your myth, not its protagonist. Love is the hero, not the man!

Over a cup of coffee I told her, 'To leave the cage door open to set free the bird of love, and go inside the cage to take its place, is a decision you have to take on your own using your mind and emotions. You alone know which bird you are waiting for. Is it a noble bird or one from a passing flock of migratory sparrows? One that pecks the seed from any proffered hand and lives off the crumbs on the table? Believe me, not every love story these days deserves all these sacrifices!'

She seemed persuaded by what I had said and mumbled, 'I think you're right. It's time for me to forget him.'

Perhaps at that very moment her heart was saying the opposite!

I have a small notebook
where I write when I forget you
a book with a black cover
I've yet to pen a word in
—Fernando Pessoa

Advice worth a herd of camels

One who warns you is like one who brings you good news

—Imam Ali

There are poems poets will never sign
There are muses who sign the life of a poet
There are writings more awesome than their writers
There are love stories more beautiful than their lovers
There are lovers who take the wrong path to love
There is a love that makes the wrong choice of lovers

There is a time not created for passion
There are lovers not created for this time
There is a love created to last
There is a love that spares nothing
There is a love as fierce as hate
There is hate to which love cannot compare
There is oblivion more present than memory

The Author, from 'Times with no Relation to the Seasons', 1986

Like no woman has loved

Only she who comes after me will bring me justice
When she empties the pockets of your heart
You will discover how rich I have made you
—the Author

Enter love an adult. Leave it a princess. Because as you enter so you will remain.

Soar upwards so that no other overshadows your stature as a lover.

In love don't give anything away cheaply, but be extravagant in everything.

Take every situation to its extreme. In excess lies your strength and makes your impact eternal. If you are moderate, you become an ordinary woman whom it is possible to forget, and replace.

Don't love him, adore him.

Don't just spend, lavish.

Don't be petty, rise above things.

Don't be reasonable, lose your mind.

Don't just live in his heart, infect it.

Don't taste him, devour him.

Don't mar anything in him, make him beautiful.

Don't be in front of him, stand behind him:

Don't be his restraint, be his impetus.

Don't be his excuse, be his goal.

Don't be his mistress, be the bride of his heart.

Don't be his rubber, be his pen.

Don't be his reality, remain his dream.
Don't always be his joy, be at times his pain.
Don't be fair, be in femininity his oppressor.
Don't cry over him, make him cry.
Don't be his pleasure, be his lust.
Be his insomnia and the princess of his sleep.
Don't be his bed, be his pillow.
Be his name amongst women.
His memories and his plans for tomorrow.
Don't be his hand, be his fingerprint.
Don't be his heart, be his entirety.
Don't be jealous of his past, for you are his future.
Nor of his family, for you are his tribe.
Don't be his watch, be his wrist.
Not his time, but his age.
Enter the mind of every woman related to him.
Every female he could ever need.
Everything he could ever touch.
Every pet animal he strokes.
Everything his eyes light upon.
Be his daughter, his cleaner and his kitten.
His prayer beads, his bath soap and his towel.
His steering wheel and his safety belt.
The lift of his building.
Be his keys and the one who opens his door, even in your absence.
Be his house robe, his prayer mat.
Be his sofa, his backrest and his silver screen.
Be his home.
Be the woman before whom there were no other women
And after whom no woman will come, only females.

Practical Advice:

Don't be amazed if he rebels against you in spite of all this, and don't be sad. Big love frightens a man who hasn't known a real woman before you. He withdraws to protect his masculinity from the flood of your femininity, and as a treatment for dissolving into you. However, I don't know a man who has been cured of cancer in the soul by taking the pill of self-deception. According to the latest studies of the heart, no one gets over big love.

Don't be jealous and don't care. Perhaps over time 'telephone girls' or 'Internet kittens' have entered his life. Perhaps women's clothes, high-heeled shoes, lipsticked kisses, breasts, perfumes and sweet-talk have passed by.

'Text messages' like no others; pleasure that tastes of candyfloss made from pure spun sugar which leaves nothing behind except a lingering stickiness. It sticks to the mouth and hands so that every time you eat it you need to take a shower.

Let them have him . . .

If you loved him like no woman has ever loved, don't cry and don't grieve. Let them enjoy him. Your happiness will be his future punishment.

As he gets older, his regret will grow with the memory of you. He might have found a woman to make forgetting you his gift, but he'll never find a woman to give him your love.

My jars are full of the tears of women
who loved you before me
but I do not cry
busy filling the baskets of laughter
for a woman who will laugh after me
at everything in you that I was protective of
—the Author

Hold out!

WHEN THE AGE IS DEGENERATE, YOU DO NOT FIND THE LOFTY SUBLIME EXCEPT IN PAIN
—Ibrahim Nagy

There is pleasure in endurance . . . even if it's a painful pleasure.

Resist the urge to surrender to the call of the past. Don't fall into the traps nostalgia sets for you. Hold out so that you remain an adult in your own eyes.

The one who abandoned you wanted to crush your dignity. So be it, you still have the pride of forgetting and the triumph of refusing to call him whatever the occasion. All the celebrations and holidays shall pass and your festive gift is to spoil the occasion for him, as long as he still ruins your life in between.

I know a friend who was creative at both times. She had broken up with the man she loved months before, and didn't call him on his birthday, despite knowing the date perfectly well, because of the years she had celebrated it with him.

Then the following year she called him on his birthday. He couldn't believe that she'd finally remembered him.

She dampened his joy, however, when she said in beguiling innocence, 'I didn't call you last year on your birthday because I still loved you and had to make an effort to stop myself calling you. But those fires have gone out since then, and now I can wish you a heartfelt Happy Birthday.'

What she really wished was to hurt him by means of a new and unexpected weapon. She left him saddened, ruing thc time when she had fought him openly . . . with her silence.

Silence can be a violent expression of suppressed love pushed to the limits; it is another extreme face of passion. When you call a man you once desired to tell him everyday things, it means that you have toppled him from his pedestal and put him on the same level as everyone else.

Silence, and the breaking of silence, are weapons every woman must master in confronting separation.

It is a lesson in patience we must perfect.

I will be patient till patience knows
I have been patient for something more
bitter than patience
—Imam Ali

The accused is innocent until hanged

We perish by what we love, we live by what we fear
—Ibrahim al-Koni

Don't station yourself by the telephone and fetter your life to it. That man has made up his mind not to call you even if you were dying, in the hope of killing you by phoniac arrest. Let him believe it!

If you want to make him happy, carry on mistreating yourself. His only objective is to torture you for a crime that only he knows. He wants to kill you in order to prove your innocence. If you are enflamed with a fascistic love, rejoice!

He is readying a pyre for you. The firewood is your stupidity.

I loved you, as if you were my last lover in the world
You tortured me, as if I was your last
enemy in the world
—The Emirati author Shahrazaad

Outdo him in love

I KNOW NO GREATER REVENGE THAN LOVE

—Unsi al-Hajj

Irrespective of his betrayal, do not submit to the urge for revenge. Only the mean-spirited think to cause harm, because it is all they are capable of. Quit the life of the one you loved like a soft breeze. Do not trash a place you once inhabited.

Do not sully the reputation of a man you loved, so that when you look backwards years later it's not ruins you find, but a garden. His retribution is in the roses that you continue to water in his garden despite not seeing them flower. Continue to protect his house, even if only with your heart. Wish him well, in the belief that, if he is decent, the good that comes to him after you will not make him forget your goodness, and that your virtue will pain and hurt him.

Be a princess.

Spoil his family members that you know without him knowing. Belittle him by outdoing him in love. Raise the threshold of generosity so that no woman would dare to come after you.

Do you know greater revenge than this?

Give generously to whomsoever you will, you'll be their prince
Be needy with whomsoever you will, you'll be their captive

—Imam Ali

'I couldn't out of self-respect'

It's not how much you love someone when you love them, but it's how much you love them when you hate them
—Ashton Kutcher

The wider the distance, the closer love becomes to a kind of painful emotional combat.

Each wants to twist the other's arm. Each gambles on longings, on the force of shared romantic habits and memories inevitably overcoming the other.

They gamble that the other will definitely be the first to give in and pick up the phone or send a text. Yet, in most cases, the magic formula betrays the lover. Absence, rather than making the hearts grow fonder, divides them for good when the days and weeks of separation become months. Then, each begins to doubt that the other loved them at all, and longing is replaced with resentment.

Here jealousy comes into its own by making insinuations to both of them that increase their stubbornness, defacing the image of the other in their heart and filling them with regret for the days they wasted.

Then, their only desire is to exact revenge for their emotional dignity; each according to their convictions, their morals, their capabilities and what they deem most hurtful to the other. This is a stupid and sadistic game of destruction that could go on for years, depending on the intensity and duration of the relationship.

It is love pushed to the extreme, to the limits of mutual destruction, as a sort of unity in fragmentation, in the manner of Kamil el-Shinawi:

Sigh for her . . . I did not realise her limits
    Sigh for me . . . She did not realise my limits
She crushed me just as I crushed her
    And she of me, and me of she, fragments

A love like this is only suitable for the ill in spirit. Love was created for us to defy the world, not for us to use to defy the one we love. It was created to build, beautify and support, not to demolish, deform and undermine. Actually, one word would have been enough. A ring of the phone, a voice surprising you and saying, 'I missed you', 'I haven't forgotten you' or 'I need you' would have been enough. But the phone doesn't ring. The love born in a cascade of beautiful words dies for the lack of one word.

Out of defiance, each lover has skimped the other a word or even a ring, simply a phone ringing. And all the while they are oblivious to the knocking on the door that might come at any moment and separate them for ever: the knock of death.

Each time you forget, it is death you remember in forgetting
— Maurice Blanchot

Giving forgetting a lift

LOVE IS THE BEST FACE-LIFT OPERATION. IT IS GENERALLY EASIER TO FIND A COSMETIC SURGEON, HOWEVER, THAN A MAN WHO DESERVES LOVE

—French actress Emmanuelle Béart

If love is the best face-lift operation, then the best anti-wrinkle cream is forgetting.

Don't allow loss to etch itself on your face as misery and wrinkles.

Romantic loss first makes itself visible on a woman's face. Whatever makeup you apply, your haggard features will give you away: eyes that haven't slept; once rosy cheeks that have been irrigated by tear canals; eyelashes, once bewitching and captivating, now broken and withered from excessive private weeping and continuous internal downpours.

First, get this man out of your face. It's imperative you don't see him in the mirror when you stand before it in the morning.

His ugliness is inside you and the harm he has caused you will turn into ugly and damaging feelings. These will install themselves in all the places in your body he occupied. His mire will flow through your veins and blood to reach your facial features.

Don't pay the price of getting this man out of your life with your beauty and freshness. He hasn't paid the added interest of breaking up, neither in time nor money. His mourning for you will be brief. For if it were long, painful and costly, he wouldn't have left you.

It's not always turning the page that's needed,
sometimes it has to be torn out
—Malik Haddad

What's he doing now?

I LIVED WITH HIM
TO SEE
HOW HE LIVES WITHOUT ME
—Hala Mohammed

There is nothing more damaging than this question: What is he doing now?

Every time you think it, you're slaughtering yourself with a blunt knife. It slays you a million times a minute. It's as destructive as the atomic bomb the Americans dropped on Hiroshima. This self-slaughter is repeated in the morning when you wake up and at night before you go to sleep, at the end of the day and at the weekend.

It happens on special occasions and on holidays, when it rains and when it snows, when the temperature rises and life's delights blossom. It's as though the calendar and nature were conspiring against you to create some need in him for a woman's presence. In each and every thing and occasion you see an opportunity for him to betray you.

This is because your memories with him give you a reference guide to his habits. You are one hundred percent certain that on the same occasions he will, if he can, repeat everything to every last detail. Men are creatures of habit.

I assure you he will. If he hasn't betrayed you yet, it's not out of fidelity to you, but out of fear of disease and the consequences of adventures. He is only looking for a safe haven for his ship. Some day his resistance will give way. He is a wounded animal easy to trap.

Women can smell him from miles away. Capturing a man with a broken heart is feminine loot. His consolation may take years, because 'the prey keeps watch on the hunter' as Talal Suleiman puts it. Whether he's the hunter or the prey, he needs someone to restore his confidence in his masculinity after you. So he will end up with casual encounters, for he lacks the patience to wait for love.

Because it is difficult for a man to make the transition from a grand passion to a little adventure, without feeling dirty or demeaning himself, he will go as far as imagining that he's in love. He will find more than one excuse to justify his actions to himself. He will accuse you of betrayal to clear his conscience. He will malign you to make himself look good. He will boycott you on the phone as if you were Israeli goods, or Dutch butter. He'll set up boycott committees among your mutual friends to support his hostile stance against you, on the basis of what he says about you without giving you a chance to respond.

In fact he no longer has a voice to confront you with. Even his voice has betrayed you.

Practical Advice:

Stop torturing yourself by asking, 'I wonder what he's doing now?'

Think a little with me: what's the most outrageous thing he could, in your opinion, do?

Well, let him do it! For God's sake, just let him do it!

Just think of all the things that he will not be able to do or have from now on – this will be the basis for his misery. As if he were himself, with his admissions and his defeats, his moments of weakness, of honesty, of revelation. Doesn't he need to put on a fine performance, to be the alpha male all the time and to pass all the tests of masculinity?

He'll no longer enjoy the bliss of holding you close until the last day of his life and become a king of the world. He has lost his throne.

And soon you'll be with someone else, and he won't be able to boast about your love anymore, not even to himself.

Tonight I can write the saddest verses
to think that she is not with me
to feel that I lost her
to listen to the vast night
vaster in her absence [. . .]
Love is often short-lived
but long long forgetting
because on a night such as this I
wrapped her in my arms
and my soul is not content with losing her
—Pablo Neruda

The line is dead

I have some time
Let me contemplate the fading of your footsteps
When love turns its back on me
Let me listen to the clamour of your absence
At this awesome moment of decline
When the telephone announces your death
—the Author

In response to the first text message that goes unanswered, stop texting him.

Total abstinence is easier on the lover than messages met by silence. Silence creates a space for interpretations that may lead you in all directions.

Chances are that you'll misinterpret the silence of the other. Some silence is meant as a reproach or an insult, another means love, and a third means counter-love. But whatever it means, it will distort the image of the other in your heart and change the way you feel about him, until he becomes alien to you. His voice is replaced by a bitterness that kills off all that was sweet between you. Whatever the message he initially wished to get across to you by his silence, it will only reach you garbled. It's an image of him.

In one of his letters the young Freud warns his fiancée of the consequences of not answering his letters and the ramifications of this for the future of their love: 'I do not want my letters to remain unanswered and I will stop writing to you immediately if you do not reply to them. A continuous soliloquy with the beloved, which does not meet with nourishment or correction, leads to mistaken ideas about the relationship. And when we meet again and find that matters are different from how we imagined them, we become like strangers to each other.'

Silence is the beginning of estrangement between two lovers who had been strangers to the whole world but not each other. Once contented with only themselves, after their break up, they become strangers to each other. It's a tragedy.

Your shock will be less if you realise this early on.

However, this realisation often comes late, because the woman continues the attempt to save love, even if only by making sporadic contact.

Practical Advice:

Nevertheless, do not open your heart (and your phone) straightaway to a new love. Allow some time for the corpse of that big love to decompose. It will be painful, but you will heal better.

Every evening consider the scene of the setting of the emotions, and the disc of love as it sinks blood red into the sea of your sorrows.

From the same place, tomorrow the sun will rise. Just as it sets inside you, so it will rise from you.

Sunset is in the mind before anything else

—Fernando Pessoa

Let him experiment!

You want to return to your youth.
Commit the same follies!
—the Author

Because we are not Sabah – the octogenarian Lebanese singer and actress one of whose seven marriages was rumoured to have been to a man fifty years her junior – as Arab women we face a major psychological barrier that makes us, whatever our age, reject younger men and go for others whose grey hairs hold out no hope.

The Arab woman, like the Arab nations, has grown up with the notion of the father-leader. Her only recognised symbol of masculinity is the ruler who grows old in power.

Therefore she does not envisage herself loving a man younger than her father the ruler. She does not understand that, in America and Russia, woman with their heads screwed on voted for leaders as youthful as Obama and Medvedev. How did the women of the world's two great powers have the audacity to abandon the closet of history and throw themselves into the arms of political youngsters?

By God, don't you find that man sleek as a black stallion – according to Berlusconi, 'handsome, youthful, suntanned' – don't you find him *sexy* when he springs onto the podium? Have you seen an Arab leader in such a rush? Don't ask yourselves why.

And that Russian lad with the elegant gait, who 'walks like a king' in the words of Umm Kalthoum, don't you find him attractive with his fine figure and wicked smile?

Some on principle and others from a complex reject younger men, even if only by a year. When we don't suffer from a mother complex, we suffer from a father complex. Sometimes we suffer from both in proof of our abundant Arabism and our femininity (you can't have too much of a good thing).

Contrary to the world's women, the Arab woman, who has grown up in a patriarchal society, does not want a young man, she wants a man straight out of the history books.

Instead she gets a man straight out of the doctor's clinic, as sedate and mature as she wants him, with grey hair and existential angst.

Yet a man in the autumn of his years needs less of loving and more of lying. The grand passion that women dream of, along the lines of Turkish soap-operas, exhausts him. We want examples of men who remain faithful lovers until the final episode.

Whereas the man has assumed a 'Mexican' frame of mind arising from soaps where you don't know whose son is whose, nor who impregnated the cleaner. He contracted swine flu from Mexican soaps, no doubt. His only treatment is quarantine with nothing but Turkish soaps until he recovers.

Don't forget that, at this age, most men suffer from heart disease, high blood pressure, diabetes, rheumatism, cholesterol, weak kidneys, vision problems, mid-life depression and . . . male problems, God preserve us from their evil.

However, between twice daily doses of medicine, between the white pills and those *blue* ones, he needs to fall in love every day. Rather than a grand passion he prefers love in easy instalments, in the belief that with every love story he becomes young again.

In fact, according to Nizar, 'A man stumbles into the first feminine hole that he encounters. The history of man is the history of falling into holes.'

Some men call 'emotional turbulence' love in their effort to evade death and old age and fearful of the final hole in the ground. In either case there is no escape.

My late friend Salih al-Azzaz, God rest his soul, would say, 'The one who grabs the tails of cows, gets thrown in the pit.'

Leave him to the cows then. I mean the 'virtuous', 'honourable', 'chaste' cows.

One day (a day closer than you think) when this creature, who like a flea – known for its attachment to cows in particular – leaps from one cow to the next, finds himself at the bottom of a hole, he will remember you fondly.

Then, when his legs have betrayed him as he tries to climb out, he will realise that he has passed the age of folly, that no medicine or magic charms will be of benefit, and that no woman other than you would have been able to save him from the pit of old age.

I shut my eyes and the world drops dead;
I lift my eyes and all is born again
—Sylvia Plath

One who falls into a river will hang on to a snake

THE MOMENTS BEFORE CATCHING A VICTIM UNAWARES ENCOMPASS MISGIVINGS WHOSE EXTENT IS KNOWN ONLY TO MEN
—the Author

The instant you fall into the abyss of separation do not resort to the first man you encounter who lends your sadness a listening ear.

This is the direst trap that men always fall into, and the most costly. For a woman who listens to a man's sorrows is halfway to his heart. It will end up with him surrendering his heart to her, in the belief that she is his mother.

It only takes seeing her – Glory to God – for his tongue to become untied and the deluge of his sorrows to be unleashed.

He will tell her his life story and divulge all his secrets, starting from his childhood and his early torments up to the most recent tale crowned by the last stupid woman before her. He made a beeline for this woman mainly to fulfil his need for an amateur psychoanalyst to listen to his confession. However, while she lends him her ear, she will be taking control of every part of him. He will not take stock of his losses until it's too late.

Her interest in him blinds him to posing questions. The answers he will discover later, when he awakes from her sedative and requires another woman to whom to bemoan what has befallen him.

You are exhausted and on the verge of drowning. You'll never distinguish between a snake and a life-ring.

There are snakes and crocodiles lurking in the river for a woman who can't swim and falls in.

You are without emotional immunity. You 'catch' love like you catch a cold or flu.

Beware of succumbing to the fate of men just re-emerging from emotional dismay. They are the easiest prey. Invariably, they fall into the snares of the first woman to take pity on them in their flight from a woman they treated badly. They optimistically hand over everything they think they have saved from the first woman. Then the second takes her revenge for the first, even if after a while. Therein, my dears, lies our consolation and the moral of the story.

A great number of stupid women must be
used to forget one intelligent woman
—Michel Audiard

Remaining faithful in the darkness of absence

Do not think your absence from us changes us
Even if distance changes lovers
By God our desires have not sought your replacement
Our hopes have not turned from you
—Ibn Zaydun

In the course of a lengthy absence, as you fumble in the dark of questions, you will be inclined towards fidelity to a lover on whose return you gamble. It's for him, at the moment of reunion, that you're holding in the release of the femininity that has forsworn life's pleasures while waiting.

Being faithful is costly; you alone set the price. Nobody knows how much you have paid, what you have turned down, how much you have waited and whether the one you waited for was worth the price.

Take your losses into consideration. Know that the recompense for your fidelity comes first in self-esteem, from taking pride in your chasteness. For chastity is a woman's jewel, and fidelity is the crown of love.

Don't expect gratitude from a lover; you may be surprised by the opposite of what you anticipated. The one you were blindly faithful to may suspect you, while another may trust a woman who cleverly betrayed him.

Being faithful these days is being clever.

What's truly amazing is that men, on account of their suffering from the Arab rooster complex, have more faith in women who lie.

They believe everything they want to hear from a woman, because it's those lies in particular that they need to hear.

The more games she plays, the greater his trust in her. He won't be on the alert except with an honest woman. Because he's a wise guy, her honesty rouses his doubts, and he's transformed into a reader between the lines, sure that what she's left unsaid is of greater magnitude.

Especially by being a wise guy, a man often loses the woman he loves and hands himself over to one who will make a fool out of him.

Didn't Lord Byron say the more you have faith in your intelligence, the easier it is for a woman to deceive you?

Pray, for in the prostration of your heart lies forgetting

IF GOD IS WITH HIM, HE LOSES NO ONE

IF GOD IS AGAINST HIM, HE KEEPS NO ONE

—Popular saying

Spiritual peace comes before romantic bliss and is more important than love. Every emotion that robs you of this peace carries the seeds of your destruction.

Fortify yourself with faith against all emotional or psychological trouble. Fight sadness with spiritual devotion. The more faith you have, the easier it will be to emerge from the trials of the heart and to win the blessing of forgetting. Because faith places you high above the injustices of men.

You ought to pray. When you pray from your heart, everyone and everything will disappear from your thoughts except God. You will transcend forgetting and reach serenity, the pinnacle of individual happiness. 'Is not in the mention of God the heart's serenity'. [Quran 13:28]

Muslim ibn Yassar was in the mosque when part of it collapsed. Although the people stood up from prayer, he did not notice that the pillar of the mosque had collapsed. He would say to his kin when entering to pray, 'Please talk to each other, I do not hear your talking.'

As for Yaqoub al-Hadhrami, his devotion went so far that he did not notice when his cloak was stolen off his shoulders, and later brought back to him, while he was still praying.

Prolong you prayers until you are no longer aware of who stole your heart, whether he takes it away or brings it back.

When you approach God in reverence, everything around you and in your heart diminishes. Every proclamation of His greatness when in His hands restores all but Him to its smallest size, reminds you that there is no Dominator but God and that every domineering man, even in love, is arrogant and of little faith. The believer is full of mercy and compassion by nature because he fears God.

Let yourself weep between the hands of God. Don't cry in the presence of a man who thinks himself a god holding sway over your life and death and bestowing you with joy and misery when he deigns.

Crying before God is devotion: complaining to anyone else is humiliation. Did you once think that you are precious to God?

Look forward to the times of prayer. God, in His majesty, awaits you five times a day. Meanwhile, there is a human creature crawling on the Earth who is too miserly to give you his voice and a kind word.

What need do you have for phone 'charity' from a mere man, when the minarets announce the call to prayer for you, and declare five times a day that the Lord of the Universe is waiting for you and loves you.

God has freed me, no one can imprison me

—Proverb

Let his devotion be a test of his heart

DEATH OF THE HEART IS RECOGNISED BY THE ABANDONMENT OF OBEDIENCE, ADDICTION TO SIN, INDIFFERENCE TO A BAD REPUTATION AND SECURITY FROM GOD'S SCHEME

—Popular saying

The outward manifestations of faith are not proof of piety. Acquire the sense of discrimination between the pious man and another who uses religion as a facade. Put the man you're interested in under the microscope to reveal his innermost thoughts.

Don't place your confidence in a man who has turned away from God after being seduced by worldly matters. One who doesn't acknowledge God's grace won't acknowledge your beauty.

One who is not ashamed of encountering God as a sinner, will sin against you without feeling guilt.

One who has grown up with prayer and fasting and gives them up on flimsy pretexts will, when he wishes, find the pretexts he needs to abandon you.

One who sees no further than his life and takes no account of the afterlife will, in love, see no further than the moment. He will not be true in his commitment to you further than a day.

One who forgets that God sees him will, when you weep at his mistreatment, forget to see your tears.

One who will not surrender before God and beg forgiveness, will pay no heed to your surrender.

One who is not driven by faith to overcome his arrogance will have tyranny as his creed.

One whose faith does not render his heart serene will be mistrustful; he will be wicked on the inside and suspicion will dwell in his heart. You will never feel secure with him.

One who has not been touched by the beauty of devotion will be disfigured by all other adornments. In the end, he will disfigure you so as not to be disgraced by you.

He is a man whose heart has died. Don't put your love in a grave, then be amazed upon separation that all that reaches your ears from him is the silence of the grave.

Recipes to forget a man

If love is gold
forgetting is diamond
There are men who enrich you with their loss

—the Author

I didn't betray you
But took to betraying time after you
I disobey the habit of obeying you
I forget that I'm waiting for you
Forget my happiness when your number appears
and fills my phone with life

Since we split up
It no longer interests me
Whether you betray me or remain true
It's all the same to me
It's enough for me, O lord of fire
that you betrayed the flame
and extinguished the smouldering minutes

I didn't betray you, but my ink betrayed you
since I decided not to write you
I just forgot to live by your schedule

I no longer remember
how many airports my heart landed in
without you knowing

The Author, from 'The Greatest Betrayal is to Forget', 2006

Keep away from the sea, and serenade it

I SEE THE SEA
WITH ITS ROUND GLASSY EYES
THOSE THAT
WERE CREATED TO CRY.
WHAT HAS BROUGHT YOU HERE?
YOU ARE TWO TEARDROPS BEFORE A WALL OF WAVES.
ALL CRYING ON THE SHOULDER OF THE SEA IS USELESS
BETTER TO WATCH IT FROM YOUR TWILIGHT BALCONY
AND LEARN TO MAKE DO WITH DESIRE'S ULTRAMARINE
—the Author

So you've made up your mind to forget. Well done, 'sister of men'.

If you want to reach the safety of the shore, don't leave dry land in the first place. Stay on the surface of things. Because if you go deep, you give feelings the chance to attack you, and you open windows that look out on more remembrance.

You want to forget; stretch out on the beach after protecting your skin with a cream against the UV-rays of longing. (Reapply the cream every two hours as per the advice of dermatologists. Longing may penetrate your pores from anywhere, because the one you love is stuck to your skin, a fact you didn't take into account, given that all Arabic songs affirm that his place is in your heart.)

This is another geo-romantic error into which the Arabs have fallen. Had we succeeded in pinpointing strategic sites, we wouldn't have lost all those wars.

Because you're not up to fateful battles, old girl, content yourself with stretching out on the beach and watching the sea from under a brightly coloured parasol. Its bright colours are part of your psychological treatment, along with the sun-bed and its comfortable cushions.

Don't, on the pretext of forgetting, set a course into your past to search sunken wrecks for your beautiful memories.

In the dark submerged world of the emotions you may be surprised by fierce sea monsters lying in wait for your descent towards the bottom without oxygen. You will meet the same fate as the poet Nizar.

The waves drag you under, you scream, 'I'm breathing under water. I'm drowning . . . I'm drowning . . . . . . '* And no one will be able to do anything for you.

The one who drowns has no voice.

Some make it and some don't!

Practical Advice:

He has fled, but he didn't take the memories with him.

They are your second retribution. You will creep into them because they are all you have left of him.

Wrong. Now you have to save your life, which he wanted to destroy.

If we assume the best of intentions, he's not interested in destroying it after he's gone. Enough diving then in search of treasure that can be salvaged from the past. When, inside the sunken ship of love, you find your lost chest of precious memories, you will have found the weapons of your mass destruction. From now on, your damnation is to live on the past, hostage to a man who meanwhile is living his present.

As long as you're alive you will have memories. So make your future memories beautiful by insisting on living.

* Lines from the lyrics of Egyptian singer Abdel Halim Hafez's '*Risala min Taht al Ma*' (A Message from Under Water) written by Nizar Qabbani.

Memories are only the accumulation of the present, as René Char puts it.

Like a goldfish
I circle ceaselessly
in the fishbowl of your love
I have no compass
just all these stupid tears
of a fish crying in the presence of the sea,
the oblivious depository of all tears
—the Author

Avoid romantic songs (unless you're a masochist)

TELL ME SEVEN SONGS YOU LOVE, AND I'LL TELL YOU YOUR LIFE STORY AND MAKE YOU CRY

—the Author

It's precisely these seven songs that you have to forget during your emotional convalescence. You will not find any solace or consolation in songs that glorify love, or those that bemoan a lover's betrayal. There is something truly amazing: when you are in love or during break ups (you're in a state, no doubt!), all songs, even the most naive, seem as though they were written especially for you. In spite of their inane lyrics, which you didn't pay attention to in the past, they will make you cry.

If you aren't a masochist, give up self-flagellation and get rid of the unnecessary pressure of random love songs.

The height of stupidity is listening to the songs you would listen to together in those happy days. How do you know, you idiot, that he's not having a nice time with someone else while you turned your house into a festival of mourning to bewail him.

Practical Advice:

Listen to music; sublime, beautiful, delightful music. Only music can beautify our sadness.

Try: The Blue Danube by Strauss; Ravel's Bolero; Clayderman's compositions on the piano; Chopin's delightful symphonies. Grieve in a cultured way, you philistine!

You should make this song by Fairouz your national anthem:

Come by, okay come by
Don't come by, then don't
It makes no difference to me
Love another, okay love another
Don't love another, then don't
It makes no difference to me
Quarrel, okay quarrel
Don't quarrel, then don't
It's not an issue

Don't believe in myths, they were written by men

THE BUTTERFLY OF THE MOMENT IS ABOUT TO FLY OFF
DON'T BE THE LAST TO ARRIVE
SOMEONE WILL COME FOR ME
AFTER THE DOOR OF MY WAITING FOR YOU
COMES OFF ITS HINGES
—the Author

Consider the millions of Arab, and other, women who have, forever and since time immemorial, wasted years of their lives awaiting the 'second-coming' of the lover.

It's only in myths and legends that the prince of your dreams returns.

Passing through the forest he spies Sleeping Beauty under the wicked witch's spell; he kisses her; she wakes up. His kiss has undone the spell. Sleeping Beauty, however, has paid for a single kiss with a hundred-years' worth of her life in a magic coma.

The story passes quickly over this waste of a woman's time. It teaches us, from an early age, to wait, be resigned and appreciate the value of what a passing man bestows. It's one kiss from him per age on the femme scale.

In the *Odyssey* Penelope is rewarded with her husband Ulysses' return. This wasn't because of her fifteen-years' work on the tapestry of waiting that, out of fidelity, she wove by day and unpicked by night. (She had told her suitors that she would not marry until she had finished weaving). But, rather, because this legend (written by a man) sought to convince women, who make up half of mankind, of the virtue of waiting for the other half. Men, like cats and farm animals, stray, wander, roam and get lost in enchanted isles. But they always return to those naive women who, in the meantime, have wasted the most beautiful years of their lives waiting as fiancées or as wives who, during the men's absence, have raised their children, preserved their honour and protected hearth and home (just as Homer would have wanted it).

If Penelope rejoiced at her husband's return after fifteen years of waiting, I know personally three stories of Arab women who waited for a jailed fiancé or husband sentenced to seventeen years in prison which end differently. When each was released, he broke up with the girl or woman he had been attached to during his imprisonment. I don't want to judge these men or blame them, given my knowledge of the psychological effects of long-term captivity, but I can only sympathise with those who spent years waiting in the prison of anticipation.

May God, who created us with vast reserves of patience and stupidity, bear witness that we are beings who have consecrated our lives to waiting to such an extent that we have forgotten exactly what it is we are waiting for, while those for whom we wait have forgotten our waiting.

It's as if in every woman's heart there is a harbour, a railway station or an airport lounge. The trains whistle, the ships sail, the planes take off; people arrive and depart while, unconsciously, she waits for the one who's coming and doesn't arrive, as though her heart were humming along with Fairouz:

You're coming but you don't arrive
Lie to me
Lying is no sin
Promise me you'll come
You're coming but you don't arrive

Practical Advice:

A little realism. Life is too short to stake on the roulette of waiting.

If he's not back in a day, he ain't never coming back. Are you sure that there isn't divine wisdom behind his being out of your life, the blessings of which you will realise later? Everything in your life happens for a reason.

Decision number one: to close down all the transit lounges in your life.

Don't leave a place for you to sit and forget yourself. Stay standing up so that your knees remind you that time's passing, as is your ability to stay standing. The one you're waiting for may have been relaxing sleeping in the meantime. I mean sleeping with someone else. He may have got married and been blessed with little ones, while you've hitched yourself to waiting.

In your promises' express
all the seats were taken
so I travelled towards you standing.
I don't like sitting
on the reserve seat of love
—the Author

Don't look far afield

FOR HIS SAKE, I LOVED ALL THAT RESEMBLED HIM
EVERYTHING ABOUT THE BELOVED IS BELOVED
—the Author

In his effort to forget you he will never go further than you. So don't search too far.

Depending on who's available and how much he longs for you or loathes you, he's with your best friend or your archenemy.

The former represents an extension of you and your punishment. It's the most painful blow. If he could, he would betray you with your sister or your mother.

The latter represents an alliance with your enemy in the search for a woman to further distort your image to him. He will be happy because, out of hatred for you, she will reassure him that he was right to dump you, or lessen his sense of loss if you dumped him. In all his relationships with women he will draw nourishment from all that resembles you: perhaps this will hurt you.

If he doesn't find either of the above, he will endeavour to love the first woman he meets from your country. She may be from your city or your region, she might even have your accent. And why not? She might share your interests, and he'd imagine that by a stroke of luck he's picked all the lottery numbers.

Memory will set traps for him in every woman who has a hint of you, or reminds him of you. He'll see in this an omen of a fateful love, and follow a new prophet in the belief that in this way he has converted from your creed. He hasn't, in fact, changed his religion or sect, just the direction of his Mecca.

Don't worry as long as you remain the original of every imitation he thinks he possesses.

Never will you forget me
Never will you forget
Eternal regret awaits you
He who lost me will end up alone
like a horse
With nowhere to tie his heart
—the Author

Don't write off his debt to your waiting

We will bankrupt ourselves in the vain
search for absolute security
—Eisenhower

Don't write off his accumulated debt to your waiting. He's not the Third World; once he was your First World, even your entire world.

If you forgive him the crime of having wasted the years of your life that have passed, you'll give him the right to plunder you again, and waste your life to come.

Be stingy in matters related to time. Your stock of it as a woman runs out fast. Your time is not valued in the same currency as his, and your patience is not weighed up as his. Your account flows into his. What he takes from the treasury of your heart will end up as part of his personal stock portfolio which, at the first signs of an emotional crisis, will crash like Wall Street in the days of the Great Depression.

All your savings, exhausted in order to acquire a house for your dreams, have gone with the wind and evaporated due to the sudden liquidation of his bank. You didn't speculate on the emotional stock exchange, but you deposited all your life's savings in a small bank, a one-man show, to which you entrusted your hopes. You didn't think of the emotions as a money market that might collapse like a house of cards. But now you have to believe that this is exactly what happened.

Practical Advice:
You have just lost everything. You have seen with your own eyes all you have amassed, penny by penny and day by day, over the course of years of amorous delusion, evaporate along with your emotional reserves. From now on learn an important lesson from bankers: don't invest all your savings in the bank of the heart.

Perhaps it was an imaginary bank, founded by a speculator playing on the stock market with small investors and idiotic women who believe they can find a rare bird among men and are ready to pay with their lives for his sake.

Have a basket of currencies. Protect yourself with reserve currencies that are controlled by the mind, not the heart.

Today, having one currency, and one face, means you're a loser. You need several tongues too, for lying, hypocrisy and cheating. No one will credit your truthfulness, or value you keeping your word. You need, my dearest, a basket of masks to deal with the man you love. He without a doubt has his masks. It will be a shock to uncover them at the end of the road.

Absorbed in ring-fencing my assets
in counting everything that convinced me
he was mine alone.
Bang. I'm engrossed counting my losses
I paste a wallpaper of sighs
in the house we'll never cohabit
—the Author

It's testosterone my dear

THE HARDEST PAIN IS WHEN THE ONLY SOLUTION
MEANS HURTING THE ONE YOU LOVE
—The late Talal al-Rashid

While fighting in defence of love, we very likely commit unforgivable sins against the one we love. We say hurtful things, the opposite of what we intend. We threaten to do what we know we never will. We claim to have done what we haven't.

Fearful of loss, or burning with jealousy, lovers do not resemble themselves. And the stronger the love, the more extreme the deformation.

You torture the other because you are tortured by him; you are tortured by the other because you still love him. It would be easier to tell him this, but you find yourself saying the complete opposite in order to hurt him.

Yet despite the pain and torment you have caused him, he will turn the tables and give you the feeling that nothing you said has hurt him. At this point, your aim will be to draw blood. For you will say things that make *you* bleed with regret. His responses will make you bleed for days, while on the other side he's haemorrhaging you.

In the face of a couple's raging destructive emotions, breaking up becomes a form of mercy killing.

That love, born at a romantic moment in the midst of bedazzlement, intoxication and the thrill of the first confession, that caused the

Earth to stand still in wonder at its advent, is now a hurricane that leaves nothing standing in its wake. It uproots all that was beautiful in love's garden and leaves the lovers' hearts exposed to the elements.

Please, stop the massacre! Don't destroy with your own hands the most beautiful memories life has given you. Don't attack each other with burning rounds of jealousy. He's the man whom you loved, who was you, before.

So be it. Let him go in peace. Time will judge between you. Years later when the fires have burnt out and the pain and the will to hurt have died, the beautiful memories will awaken. This love of yours may become a wonderful companion for the rest of your life.

Especially in this situation, put yourself to the test, strengthen your will and resist your feminine tendency to snap, even if the reasons are purely hormonal.

Since I can detect the whiff of men spying on us between these pages, I will address them directly to explain that a woman's hostility does not come from her bad temper. But because love makes her that way. Scientific research has determined that when a woman falls in love her level of testosterone – the masculinising hormone linked to the aggressive tendency – rises. (This discovery might prompt you to be distrustful of a woman who treats you kindly, acts compliantly and agrees with you about everything. Alternatively, it might reassure you that women's emotions, of the fierce Arab sort, are true.)

The same study went on to say that when men fall in love, their testosterone levels drop, and they become kind, refined, emotional and sensitive. Before this research was published, Roland Barthes had already said, 'When a man loves, he is imbued with femininity.'

Must we conclude that a man who suddenly starts treating us with aggressive machismo has stopped loving us?

Must men realise that a woman who no longer replies to their texts wildly and savagely, but politely and sweetly, has made up her mind to direct her savageness towards another man?

Let men be happy with the anti-love love that women deploy at them. Love will never be more honest than when it fires words randomly at you.

One day, the shots will be aimed at the chest of another man; the dead man will be the one who hopes for a bullet to revive him. But forgetting has already killed him in this woman's heart.

When a woman hates a man to death,
know that she used to love him to death
—Mark Twain

Chocolate is your weapon

STRENGTH IS THE CAPACITY TO BREAK A CHOCOLATE BAR INTO FOUR PIECES WITH YOUR BARE HANDS – AND THEN EAT JUST ONE OF THE PIECES

—Judith Viorst

Femininity means mood swings, rebel emotions, extreme feelings, a permanent hunger for sympathy and a thirst for towering desires for which women have no name.

No one is going to come along and pull you out of your sadness and depression, your sense of failure, your loneliness and emotional disappointments; except, that is, for chocolate.

That delectable dark curse melts in your mouth, reprograms your mood for the better and fills you with ecstasy. It leaves an aftertaste of its delight as if it had erased what came before.

Chocolate is woman's friend. It is compensation for all her losses and solace for all her disappointments. Women will go as far as giving up a basic pleasure to enjoy a chocolate bar. According to a survey, a majority of Canadian women preferred having chocolate to having sex.

Perhaps these two pleasures are related. Mexican monks, six centuries ago, banned women from eating chocolate when they realised its sexually arousing effect. The Spaniards, the first westerners to discover cocoa, limited its consumption to the nobility and soldiers on account of its fortifying contents.

We can, then, in our battle with the past and against painful memories arm ourselves with chocolate. For it can effortlessly help us to overcome heartache and resist our tendency to depression at the painful endings of love affairs.

Choose it dark, with few calories. Dark chocolate is more effective, more delicious and has a more potent effect on the mood. This is provided you don't eat too much and get hooked. Then you may need skin patches to get cured!

The best cure is for you to find a darling man to give you chocolicious words to taste when you wake up and when you go to bed. Words that make you melt or are themselves melted and spoon-fed to you.

Look around you: there are lots of men looking for a feminine vessel to pour their passion into. Like that lover who gave his beloved a chocolate dress moulded to measure. I don't know whether he stripped it off her with his hands or his teeth, and whether after devouring her coating, he still had the ability to devour her.

Love for men: a side dish; love for women: a full banquet
—Roland Barthes

The shortest route to forgetting

LOVE DESCENDS ON A WOMAN AT A MOMENT OF
CALM FILLED WITH DOUBT AND WONDER
—H. G. Wells

Some of the women around me have accused me of offering utopian advice. They have reproached me for ignoring the shortest and most worthwhile piece of advice to forget a man. I will not go into this 'mother of all advice'. Particularly given that it is possible to summarise it in one sentence. That would relieve the need for everything in this book. A book I wrote to help the patient and sensible among you stand up to gales of memory and storms of longing.

Nevertheless, I cannot completely ignore it due to its practicality. Equally, I do not wish to be held responsible for its consequences. Therefore, you will have to discover it on your own, in the same way that Archimedes, immersed in his bathtub, discovered his principle. He then ran out of the bathroom shouting, 'Eureka! Eureka!'

You can imitate his experiment. Fill the bath and relax in the bubbles and bath-oils. Light some candles and play some mood music. Fill your thoughts with the shortest way to forget a man. Like Archimedes, perhaps inspiration will strike you in the bath!

Who knows?

All the same, let me draw your attention to a mistake I fear you might make and then blame me for your sins.

Your senses should be wide awake when you are seeking 'the

mother of all advice'. This is because the answer, clever girls, is not the very first thought that comes to mind (and that strikes a chord) but, unfortunately, the second!

A little deliberation please! The essence of intelligence, my dears, is to distinguish between the first thought and the one immediately after, which is where your salvation lies.

May God help you, and good luck!

My darling
What are we doing in this homeland
that is afraid to see its body in the mirror
lest it desire it
and is afraid to hear a woman's voice on the phone
lest its ablutions be polluted
—Nizar Qabbani

Just like men forget

THE BEST WE CAN EXPECT OF MEN IS FORGETTING

—François Mauriac

I had a recurring wish: if only her voice was on sale in the pharmacies for me to buy. I need her voice to live. I need a dose of it three times a day: on an empty stomach, before bed and when sadness or happiness overwhelm me like now.

What is this science that is so far unable to encapsulate the voice of the one we love in pills or shots for us to take secretly when we are afflicted by an emotional indisposition, whose cause does not know how much we need them.

Bed Hopper, 2003

The vicious silence of men

WE HAVE STOPPED TALKING WITH THOSE WE LOVE:
THIS IS NOT SILENCE
—René Char

A woman's weapon is her tears, or so say the men who cannot defend themselves by crying along. Men, however, have discovered a weapon not found in a woman's armoury. Women don't know how to confront it, because their psychological make-up makes them incapable of it. When a man brandishes it in her face, her antennae get crossed and her radar breaks down. She is struck by the blindness of femininity in the glare of a man who has chosen to stand in the dimness of silence.

No woman can interpret a man's silence nor understand the message it's supposed to relay. This is especially so if she loves him. Love is itself another form of blindness. (When she stops loving him, neither his words nor his silence matter. This is where a man can make the mistake of continuing to use this weapon off the battlefield against a woman when she's no longer in range.) Similarly, for some sufferers from emotional ambivalence, silence becomes a scourge to punish you with, but ends up punishing him.

The power of men's silence lies in its being a weapon for misleading. It's like the camouflaged kit worn by soldiers so they can blend into any battleground. The camouflage adopts the tone of any space they move in.

It is the silence of the chameleon – if the chameleon had a voice. Its tones vary from one feeling to its opposite, and a woman stands before it in confusion, all the possible interpretations flitting through her mind.

The silence of passion; the silence of defiance; the silence of pain; dignified silence; insulting silence; indifferent silence; soothing silence; the silence of one soothed; the silence of lovesickness; the silence of one who wants to keep you infected by him; the silence of one confident that he alone has your medicine; the silence of one who bets that you'll be the first to break the silence; the silence of one who wants to break you; the silence of a couple who have loved to the point of breaking; vengeful silence; cunning silence; deceitful silence; abandoned silence; disappointed silence; the silence of forgetting; the silence of great sorrow; arrogant silence; the silence of one who has betrayed you; the silence of one who believes you have betrayed him and wants to kill you with silence; the silence of one who believes you will dump him one day, and so leaves you in the wilds of silence; preventative silence; guilty silence; raging silence; the silence before the storm; the silence of melting; the silence of whirlwinds; silence as the vegetative state of love; silence as another state of love which joins two lovers until death; the silence after which nothing follows; and the silence that redeems that nothingness and gives rebirth to beautiful pure everlasting things after silence has cleansed them of love's faults.

Silence is a choice. Blessed are those who come through it however long it lasts. They attain the crown of eternal love, or the laurels of freedom.

Practical Advice:

Learn to differentiate between adult silence and mega-silence. Adult silence is assessed by its effect; big silence by its extent.

Adults say in the silence between two sentences, or in the silences during a romantic dinner, what others do not say in months of silence. Silence, in order to be silence, needs speech at some moment to break it.

As for open-ended silence leading to more silence, it intimates weakness or an emotional defect concealed behind a mask of silence from fear of confrontation. Only one who knows exactly when silence ought to be broken and who chooses the words in between two silences like a jewel smith is capable of adult silence.

Learn to listen to the silence of the one you love, and not just his words. It is only silence that reveals a man's mettle.

Do you hear my longings
when I am silent?
Silence, my lady,
is my most potent weapon.
Have you felt the splendour of
what I say
when I say nothing?
—Nizar Qabbani

Confronting telephone starvation

WHEN HE FINISHES POLISHING HIS SHOES
WITH THE KOHL OF YOUR TEARS
AND AFTER HE'S DEODORISED
AGAINST THE SWEAT OF MEMORY
HE MAY REMEMBER
AND PHONE YOU . . . LORD OF ALL PHONE CALLS!
—the Author

One day, with no warning, the phone will announce an open-ended emotion-strike. This is after the feasts of love and all the rich dishes of passion he laid before you. (So much so that you suffered emotional indigestion and an outbreak of spots.) Now you have to try the 'phone diet' and emotional indigence.

You're broke and starving, in need of a single telephonic 'unit' from him to keep body and soul together. You'll go to sleep every night hungry. You'll cook dream stew, like that Bedouin woman* who boiled stones to feed her children, in order to sleep.

You still do not have strength, and do not know how long your starvation will continue. The declaration of a sustenance embargo against you is the sign for you to make up your mind to give up the telephone drip that you have been attached to for months and that has been turned off to kill you.

* A reference to the story of the woman in Medina who was boiling water to 'feed' her starving children when Caliph Omar Ibn al-Khattab visited during his regular nocturnal rounds.

Expect, therefore, to be made miserable at the end of every love affair. You will never believe what's happening to you.

But in time, you'll wake up and decide to pull out this drip-feed to your heart and come back to life. You'll still have some plasters on where it hurts, but you will refuse to live at the mercy of the phone ringing.

It's the right decision. Refuse to allow a man to grace you with a 'mercy ring' as a form of mercy killing.

Let him go to Hell.
The man expecting my phone call
Anxiously awaiting my voice
Has a mobile in his pocket
But my pocket holds his heart
—the Author

That device that demeans us

IN THE TWENTIETH CENTURY LOVE IS A PHONE THAT DOESN'T RING
— French saying

Maybe the problem began the day people in this crazy, frantic age forgot the language of the eyes, the first human language to convey feelings. Even in films, people no longer exchange those long captivating looks.

I remember my great friend Nour el-Sherif telling me once, 'A true actor is one whose eyes speak his lines before he does, so that sometimes he doesn't even need to say them.' The famous Egyptian actor could have been talking about a true lover.

Just today I read an interview with the great American director Steven Spielberg who said that the day we stop talking with our eyes will be the end of society. Have we come to this end because we have started to speak the language of the telephone, the television and the Internet? Because we swap longings via text and TV messages, and in chat-rooms, without making eye contact? Our eyes are glued to the screen; our hearts are stuck on a device that manipulates our moods and feelings.

Today, the definition of love is no longer, 'Two people looking in the same direction', but two people looking at the same device. Joy is no longer meeting the one we love, but getting a text from him.

Since we handed our romantic destinies over to machines, grand romantic passion has died and given way to these small pleasures of technology, which come and go at the press of a button.

The beautiful age of waiting for the postman is over.

No more mail box whose key we kept in secret and which we raced to get to before anyone else.

No more letters that we learnt by heart and treasured for years. No more excuses to be found for the lover whose letter was delayed or who hasn't written.

Today we know his message hasn't got lost and hasn't been delayed.

It's now possible for a lover to calculate in minutes the period of demeaning silence between a text and its reply.

Whenever I kiss you
after a long time apart
I feel that
I'm putting an express love letter
in a red post box
—Nizar Qabbani

The phenomenon of men's sudden disappearance

TELL ME, MAN:
TO WHICH CLOUD DO YOUR LIPS BELONG?
TO WHICH STORMS DO YOUR HANDS BELONG?
IN WHICH DIRECTION ARE YOUR INTENTIONS HEADED?
TELL ME SO THAT I CAN TRAVEL IN THE SUITCASE OF YOUR RAIN
AND ALIGHT WHEREVER YOU POUR
—the Author

He will disappear. Anticipate this from his first appearance in your life.

A man is a comet that will disappear from your sky without a warning from any astronomical observatory. What you'll need then is to become an astrologer, or learn geomancy or I Ching. It is most important when you start a relationship, to know some form of divination. Logical thinking will be of no help at all when it comes to finding the answers that will give you insomnia in the future.

Like the fortune tellers of your mother's time – not those of today's computerised astrology – you must wrap a scarf round your head and sit in front of a crystal ball to follow the paths of the galaxies and planets that the comets of men orbit.

Alternatively, according to an Arab woman's recipe for white magic, melt a piece of lead in a small iron pot. When it turns to a silvery liquid, place an iron mortar containing seawater between your knees and pour the molten liquid into the mortar. The water will splash out in proportion to the quantity of evil and envy in your life. The molten lead will solidify and form strange shapes. You have to solve their riddles and interrogate their smallest details and protuberances: 'Where has the creature disappeared to?'; 'And God forbid with whom?' Or read the coffee grinds asking, 'When will fortune shine on me and he return?'

Because you have no knowledge of magical formulae, and God has only graced you with questions (answers are in the metaphysical realm and with the psychologists specialising in men), you will spend days exhausting yourself by going over every word he said, or you said, during the final phone call. Perhaps you will discover the magic word after which he vanished from sight.

You require one of those black boxes that hold the secret of the final moments in a plane crash. Was the breakdown in the relationship caused by 'human error' or a 'technical fault'. Did love's fuel run out, or was there a fateful collision with another love that destiny had kept hidden from you or him?

Practical Advice:

Don't dissipate your energy with questions. Be fatalistic. Don't run after a fleeting comet: there are many more stars in the sky.

How do you know, perhaps in the love to come you'll find your destiny is the moon.

Timid as a squirrel
I leap between your branches
I don't know in what cleft
to hide the chestnut of joy.
How often you said:
'You're the only woman for me'
but in every cleft of a tree
I find the corpse of a woman
who had you before me
—the Author

Let the rabbit run

THE WAY TO FIGHT A WOMAN IS WITH YOUR HAT –

GRAB IT AND RUN

—John Barrymore

You should know, God have mercy on you, that man is a rabbit: at the first sign of trouble he runs. Because his behaviour is unjustifiable and your many questions unanswerable, running away provides him with an honourable way out.

He simply walks away. That's what he calls it to himself; you can call it what you will, for he won't be around to argue over words.

Where does he run to? Take comfort; he doesn't always run to another woman. To begin with, like a hunted or wounded animal, he'll escape to his den.

He'll pull himself together and catch his breath; he'll organise his papers; he'll be jubilant at his freedom and at having saved his manhood from what he sees as a women's, or emotional, trap. But he won't be totally happy. He'll need some time to stand firm in the face of the gusts of nostalgia that take him backwards.

After this, he will gradually come back to life. His limbs will start to gyrate like a beetle flipped onto its back. He will flounder for a while searching for another woman to help him stand on his feet. When he finds her (I mean when she finds him) the same fears will grip him, and he will repeat the rabbit ploy with her.

Practical Advice:

Don't be sad on account of a rabbit who has done a runner on you. A man who has run once, will run every time from every woman.

Be the first to run from such a man so as not to give him the chance to waste your time or demean you. Reverse the law of masculinity and be the one to demean him by walking away. Only then will you become his 'bunny' complex, and he'll start chasing after you.

Men love you when you demean them.
Don't ask why, that's how they are
—Pamela Anderson

Man, that being that never apologises!

WHEN IT COMES TO THE BIG THINGS MEN PRETEND AS IT PLEASES THEM. IN THE SMALL THINGS THEY APPEAR AS THEY REALLY ARE
—Comte de Chambord

The Arab man needs to put you in the dock in order to grant you forgiveness and become your 'lord and master'.

A man is a mini Arab ruler whom circumstances have not permitted to rule a people. But God has put you in his path: you are his people.

You should know, then, that you will never hear a word of apology from him as long as you live, no matter what sins he commits against you. He has wasted years of your life, perhaps your whole life, dissipated your energy to work, crushed what might have been your greatest achievements. He has held sway over your stock of emotions and your bank of feelings and squandered them all before your very eyes. In spite of this you will not be able to hold him to account.

Has a single Arab people brought a ruler to justice for his misappropriation of wealth that he acts as if he's inherited from his father? In the same vein, don't expect an apology from your man. Have you ever seen an Arab leader apologise to his people? Do you expect a man to apologise for lying to you or breaking his electoral pledges (when you were engaged), or pilfering your dreams and expending them on another, for getting caught in flagrante delicto;

just as the press caught Bill Clinton with his trousers down, trai
Monica in the White House?

You are blessed with a democratic love. You have the right to listen to a man who, instead of apologising for his abuse and suspicion of you, will wait for your apology for something you know nothing about born of his imagination and his masculine fears and doubts. Just like every Arab ruler, the amorous Arab is paranoid. He expects only plots and treachery from those closest to him.

Expect him to punish you for long weeks and months until you submit to him on your knees.

Practical Advice:

Every defence on your part will be used against you. Keep shtum: don't swear oaths or cry and put yourself in the role of the accused.

By such behaviour you confirm to him that he is right and you are guilty.

Talking in particular is no use. He will not believe anything you say. Does a despot believe one who says he deeply and truly loves him?

Steer clear of a man who lacks the courage to say sorry. So that you don't one day lose your self-respect, by forgiving him his insults and wrongs against you for which he sees no need to apologise. He will repeat them over and over while his contempt for you grows.

If men knew the majesty of a manhood that admits mistakes, they would garland themselves in apologies.

The ethics of a man should be gauged by this: Does he see owning up to his mistakes as a virtue or as a blow to his dignity?

True manhood means seeing when all other eyes are blind;
it is the civilization of a word in the presence of silence;
it is an arm stretched forth to protect, a mind that thinks to
preserve and a heart that beats to forgive

—Mohammed al-Sayyid Mohammed

Forgetting, not love, is the man of your life

LOVE KILLS TIME WHILE TIME KILLS LOVE
—Popular saying

We spend our lives flirting with love and making ourselves beautiful in preparation. We sacrifice ourselves for it when it comes, accommodate ourselves to its capricious moods, make its disasters look good and ignore its complications and its flaws.

We make the most beautiful room in our heart ready for it, then waste no time in giving it our whole heart as a furnished flat while we wander homeless without refuge. Love is an occupation we are content with. We ask him in as our occupier and our dictator in the belief that he is the ideal, most desirable and eternal man of our life.

Then, in exchange for a few days' happiness, we pay the price in months and years of misery. No one told us that love is transient, that it stays a while then continues on its way without you, however long the journey. (Whereas forgetting stays throughout our days and in our beds and diaries. *It* is the man of our life.)

If that's how it is, why don't we prepare for forgetting, make ourselves beautiful to receive it, celebrate it and pamper it? It is our only true support in this world.

If we think logically, shouldn't we be ashamed of failing to give forgetting its due. Isn't it bad enough that we have created a holiday for love and forgotten to celebrate forgetting, when it's forgetting that comes along every time to rescue us from the injustice of love? If love has St. Valentine's Day, consistency requires that forgetting has a time or season of which it is lord and master.

As long as we fail to give forgetting its due, love will continue to get the better of us and treat us like a dog (as we say in Algeria), that is, like a dog treats its food. It tips over the bowl with its paw, mixes the food together and plays with it before eating it up.

Whereas forgetting gives us healthy organic food to keep us well and save us from emotional food poisoning.

Every day memory sets a trap for me out of the details of my past

—Adonis

'Yes We Can'

DREAM LOFTY DREAMS, AND AS YOU DREAM,
SO YOU SHALL BECOME
—James Lane Allen

If Obama could achieve the miracle of changing the lot handed to him by history, going from the descendant of an African slave to the president of the world's most powerful state – among whose citizenry are those whose ancestors owned his – then you can also do away with a man's enslavement of you, forget the marks of his fetters around your wrists and start making something of your life. Freedom means not waiting for anyone.

Slavery is nothing more than being willing to put yourself in a position of waiting for a man who is nothing more than a slave to his commitments and obligations, among which love is not always a priority.

Freedom means being free to choose your own chains, which may be tighter than those imposed by another. It is the emotional and moral discipline that you impose on yourself and champion like a bill of rights.

Freedom means the severity with which you hold yourself to account and your refusal to render accounts to a man who insists on being your master and your angel of death, who has an inventory of all your sins while you haven't the slightest knowledge of his mistakes.

Learn to distinguish between bonds and handcuffs. Refuse the latter even if they are diamond encrusted (like those a rich man gave his beloved and which were specially designed on the pattern of those the police put round the wrists of criminals). Your acceptance of them, even out of passion for your lover, will lead you to enter emotional detention camps on charges that are known only to the mind of your jailer.

Remember that chains don't protect love but destroy it, because they are not proof of it but evidence of doubt. However much you long for your jailer, one day you will break his chains.

'The night inevitably ends and the chains inevitably break', said the Tunisian poet Abul Qasim al-Shabi in his masterpiece 'If One Day the People Will to Live'.

Rescue us by elephant

THE WORLD HAS TAUGHT ME:
NOT ALL WOLVES ARE ENEMIES
NOT ALL BIRDS ARE FRIENDLY AND NOT ALL RABBITS TAME
NOT ALL LIONS FEROCIOUS
NOT ALL CHILDREN INNOCENT
NOT ALL FOXES CUNNING
NOT ALL SCORPIONS POISONOUS
NOT ALL DOGS FAITHFUL
—The Emirati writer Shahrazaad

In the book *Les hommes et les femmes*, which takes the form of a dialogue between writer Françoise Giroud and French philosopher Bernard-Henri Lévy, Lévy states that the finest that has been said about faithfulness he read in a text by Françoise de Salle where she says, 'Man resembles the elephant, who never desires to replace the mate he has chosen. This giant beast is the most loyal creature on Earth. Imagine two spouses faithful to each other for fear of catching AIDS: what is the value of such faithfulness? Only the fidelity of the mystics is true. They are the faithful of the first order. Because they realise their weakness and resolve to remain firm. This is the finest and most sublime form of faithfulness.'

Millions of women around the world dream of meeting this mystic who has renounced all the women of the world and thinks only of one woman, the one he has chosen as his beloved for life.

So as not to do an injustice to men, we say that among them there exist some true lords of loyalty. Men as loyal as prophets to their mission, beautiful in chastity and generous in their love – except these grand emotions of theirs also engender grand doubts. They do not trust the emotions of the other party and do not expect a woman could match, or even exceed, them in fidelity.

Unfortunately, such people usually create their own torture. They lose the love of their life and are extinguished inside for ever, because they were created for grand passion and their hearts baulk at accepting emotional crumbs. They are not sparrows: they are eagles. The eagle being the other creature that is content with one mate and remains faithful to her as long as he lives.

If life gifts you this noble bird as a lover, it is your chance to live the legend of grand passion. Treasure him with patience towards his abuse. Give the lie to his doubts by loyalty. Stay faithful to him however long the separation. The noble bird always returns.

Should life only send you the cheats and liars among men, then find an elephant to love!

True, you'll need to travel to India or Africa to find your other half. But are you confident of finding a loyal man where you are? For fidelity is on the decline and the temptations of betrayal on the rise.

Plus with an elephant, besides his faithfulness, you are assured he'll never forget you. Memory is the prime characteristic of elephants (something not found in eagles which in turn possess eyesight five times sharper than humans; so you will have to take into consideration his acute vision. This means not neglecting to attend to the smallest details of your femininity and keeping the wax hot on the stove night and day. His gaze won't miss a single stray hair!)

Imagine how fortunate you would be with an elephant! You can boast to your friends that you have found a faithful creature who won't forget you in a lifetime. All women will be obsessed with him but he will never cheat on you with another woman. If he can hardly even see you, how can he be led astray by another? It's well known that he advances waving his trunk in all directions, not looking where he's going. Expect then to win a loyal being who will smash everything in your life, from whence the expression, 'he came into my life like an elephant comes into a china shop'. Don't worry about the destruction he leaves behind, his memory intercedes on his behalf.

Isn't the ability to forget our first complaint against men?

Believe me, I see the elephant as the only way to achieve our demands. I mean within the bounds of his capabilities. With a view to size, we would not go as far as asking him to use all of them. Personally, I wouldn't recommend anything sexual, for with regard to this creature it's not in a woman's interest to flirt with him, to avoid being confined to bed for twenty-two months (the gestation period of the female elephant). Although, with regard to myself, this might be my only opportunity to stay at home and finish the rest of my oeuvre. I might then come up with a major novel and produce for you, rather than a mouse, an elephant!

It would be a catastrophe after this if the elephant, which enjoys a vengeful memory, should forget that I am his mate and the mother of his offspring. For he would start his retribution for my betrayal of him in my novels and might go mad with rage, in the process fulfilling the wish of some writers of both genders for my demise crushed under his feet in a bout of jealousy!

In this case I would have 'escaped death only to fall into the grim reaper's arms', as my mother puts it.

Practical Advice:
Life: it's a jungle out there. (I've spent my life finding that out.)

As you advance in years you become more caught up in the bush and find yourself compelled to deal with beasts in human form, especially if you're a butterfly of a woman who imagines that the world is a meadow of flowers. You should take note that every being you see, man or woman alike, hides another being. 'We live in a jungle most of whose animals live inside us.'

We only differ in terms of the species we are descended from. Among us are horses, peacocks, snakes, dolphins, foxes, scorpions, canaries, dogs, cats, elephants, giraffes, lions, rabbits, mice and pigs. You ought to acknowledge the animalistic traits in each person, before you hand yourself over to them. Before you say hello to them even. Perhaps he was a frog who turned your greetings into a story to croak in the swamps.

Perhaps you imagined him an eagle. But he turned out to be one of those vultures that wait for the right moment to swoop down on you.

Perhaps you imagined him a dolphin and went swimming and playing with him. But he turned out to be a shark with his jaws open to devour you. Perhaps you imagined him a dog. But he turned out to be a wolf. Or you thought he was a Siamese cat, and in your house he turned into a ferocious lion.

It has become necessary for us to learn the science of physiognomy. We have to give up watching current affairs and music channels in exchange for nature programmes so that we don't get it wrong when choosing the 'animal' of our life.

Enough disappointments!

Women and elephants never forget
—Dorothy Parker

The ambushes of memory

MEMORY IS THE MIND'S BEST SERVANT, FORGETTING IS THE HEART'S

—Popular saying

There are no dead apart from those we bury in the graveyard of memory. By the act of forgetting we are able to hold a funeral for whomever we wish of the living, then wake up in the morning and decide they are no longer here.

We can fabricate their death in writing, invent their end with a stroke of the pen, startlingly in a car crash, shockingly drowned. It no longer concerns us whether they remain alive after. We do not want their death; we want to mourn the corpse of their memory, like we mourn for the dead. We need to get rid of their things, their presents, their letters, our memory's entanglement with them. We need to go into mourning rapidly and briefly, and then forget.

To get over an amorous condition, you require the rubble of love, not the statue of a lover you keep polishing after breaking up, hooked on that gleam that once captivated you. You require a grave, a headstone and the courage to bury the person once closest to you.

Bed Hopper, 2003

Do you really want to forget?

OPEN WIDE YOUR ARMS, MY MEMORY,
FOR IT IS TIME TO WELCOME FORGETTING
—Nadia Tueni

Since you decided to forget him you've been plagued by a pain that you can't locate.

Exactly where this man lived inside you up till now, you do not know. Every part of your body hurts since you decided that from now on he has no place in your life. You understand the meaning of Nizar's words, 'I severed the roots of your love in the hidden depths.'

Pain isn't found on the surface. It's in your nerve endings, your joints and your cells.

Everything in you weeps for him and despises him. It makes you cry and rebels against you; you are your opponent and the referee, the decision and the pain. You have to decide resolutely: do you really want to forget? Even when you answer yes, ask yourself again, in the manner of Chris Tarrant, 'Final answer?'

On this subject, expect to change your answer more than once, even after the allotted time.

For this question in particular, don't ask the audience or phone a friend. They won't be around when, night and day, you hurl yourself into the bitterest battles of your life against memory, that is, against yourself.

What you would love to do, specifically, is amputate parts of yourself and swap them with new human spare parts which have no connection with your past and whose memories are blank. You want to exchange memory for forgetting, which is alien to you and which your body will reject to begin with. You will manifest the physiological and psychological symptoms that accompany such conditions.

If you intend to forget, enter the battle and give time some time. The body even manages to accommodate an artificial heart beating inside. Who knows? Perhaps you'll be the first Arab woman to succeed in this experiment.

Your body is a major linguistic conundrum
I do not know how to conjugate it
nor how to forget it
—Nizar Qabbani

Leaving behind what gives us away

O BOUNTIFUL IN ABSENCE

—Saeed Aql

Giving is one of love's pleasures, and one of its yardsticks.

When a man loves you – I mean when he adores you – he wishes he could share all he has with you or, rather, cede you all he owns and become reliant on your hospitality, in the belief that he has no abode and no property in the world apart from you.

There are some whose generosity exceeds their means, because their hands are in competition with their heart. They will give you in a matter of days what others would not give over the course of years. It will be hard for you to forget a generous man (just as it is difficult for a man to forget a generous woman).

After him, objects will keep reminding you that he left a piece of his heart in everything around you. His generosity was not intended to bribe your heart, but to make you happy on account of his ultimate happiness in you.

His presents had no special occasion; just daily gratitude to life for placing you in the path of his heart. It's as though he had wanted to enwrap you completely so that everything you touched, be it expensive or cheap, only came from him.

It's as though he wanted to relieve you of every burden, every concern worrying you. His outpour overwhelmed everything around you. No dam can withstand the force of a man who loves you madly. The most dangerous thing about him is that he will become your benchmark for love, not on the scale of his pocket, but on the scale of his heart. For the value of a gift is in what a man spends of himself, not the money he spends. You will ask yourself whether those who passed through without leaving behind anything tangible that attests to their passage through your house, your wardrobe and your celebrations, really did love you.

You wouldn't notice that a man you loved for years hasn't left a single thing behind him, unless you missed him madly once he left, and then tried to seek solace for his absence in his things. But you haven't found anything of his to touch or to wear.

How you long to wear what he gave you, to surround yourself with his mementos. Anything of his would suffice to meet your emotional needs for months.

But he has left you a wilderness without things. Even so you should be happy. There isn't a single thing around you or on you that will remind you of him or torment you with his memory. Nothing that you touch, that you smell, will make you cry. Nothing will conspire with him against you and arouse your yearning.

Over time you will find consolation in your being free of him. Doing without is the beginning of forgetting.

Maybe he wasn't a miser or self-centred. Maybe he was generous with priceless things. But he wasn't interested in surrounding you with them as much as he was concerned with possessing you.

A French lady relates that when she could find nothing to feel from the man who had dumped her, and knowing that he had a pet cat at home, she got a kitten. She would sit the cat in the place where her lover sat. Whenever she missed him, she would put the cat in her lap and stroke its fur. The cat would submit to her caresses and fall asleep. She would be happy at times, and at others cry.

Over time the cat became 'the man of her heart'. It recognised her steps, awaited her return by the door, followed her from room to room. She fed it and pampered it and doted on it, and it returned her kindness with loyalty and affection.

When our cat died a while ago, I recalled this woman and asked myself what if her cat dies one day? For which one of the triangle would she shed tears: herself, her lover or the cat? Which of the two of them would die in her heart first, and for which would she mourn?

Which, then, of these two alternatives is a greater betrayal and humiliation of manhood: for a woman to seek help from one man to forget another, or to resort to a cat to make her forget a man, when she found nothing of his left to help her wait?

What times are these when a grand passion ends up as an emotional commitment to a cat? A man betrays a life together and a woman devotes herself to an animal, her disappointment leading her to renounce the species of men.

He's intent on your spiritual assassination

If my beloved wanted my perdition
He'd obtain his aim from me far beyond his aim
—the Author

Forgetting is the corpse of the days of love laid out between two ex-lovers.

It is waiting's senseless brain death; waiting that you imagined would last one day but soon turned into a week, then a month, then an eternity, for a totally unknown reason.

It is the gradual obliteration of the functions of all your betrayed body parts. The death of sensation for all your senses, which broke down with the breakdown of your internal clock that ran according to love time.

It is memory, ticking like a clock inside you, that draws your attention to former habits murdered by a man who has declared your spiritual assassination. A clock whose hands he was, only to become its toll.

Each time you wait for his voice at that fixed time and it doesn't come, you die a little more from silence poisoning. His venom gets into you from the corpse of the telephone.

Your sense of his ingratitude towards your loyalty and his indifference to your pain doesn't leave you; neither does his dismissal of the possibility of you dying from suffering after time itself has died, and he too has died inside you, poisoned by jealousy.

These are painful feelings that will gnaw away at you and finish you off in a matter of minutes. You will be too tormented to be aware that his venom is exactly the prescription you need to get over him, and that God, who loves you, has inspired him to be the means of your emancipation.

Day after day, your body will get used to the doses of poison, and it will no longer have an effect on you. He has inoculated you against addiction to him. Of course this was not his planned intention. Perhaps he thought that you would, in the fashion of desperate addicts, hold up a pharmacy and, threatening violence, get hold of your hit of 'love's cocaine' by asking for pills of his voice, the serum of those words of his. Or that you would take two lovers hostage and threaten to kill them if he doesn't turn up, to spite love.

Or you may take pity on them and decide to kill yourself to spite him. You leave behind a message of love and loyalty to your abuser on the off chance that your death will make him miserable for the rest of his days.

These are his unspoken wishes. He wants tangible proof of how crazy for him you are. But you, who really were crazy about him, shall restore your mental powers in the face of this challenge.

In our day, Qais is no longer the crazy one; every 'Qais' is interested in finding his crazy woman.

'May God increase the idiots, so the sensible can prosper,' as my mother would say.

Get well as soon as you can. Remember that a love whose venom feeds on your goodness and patience is not love, but a pathology.

The more our love grows, the more we fear hurting the one we love

—Balzac

The scent of forgetting

PERHAPS MY PERFUME HAUNTS YOU
MY EMBRACE DETAINS YOU
AND ALL WOMEN DISAPPOINT YOU
SO BROKEN IN SPIRIT YOU COME BACK TO ME
—the Author

Forgetting has no scent. The scent can only be the scent of memories.

I stumbled across this truth while looking for a perfume for absence, to save us from the perfume of memory that is emotionally linked to what we lived and shared with someone.

This does not seem easy. Humans have 347 genes relating to the sense of smell compared with only four for sight. That is we see, love, crave, long, eat and remember with our noses.

Scent is a mix of the chemistry of the body and the chemistry of the perfume in its bottle. Thus there are as many perfumes as there are people.

Every woman should create the magical blend for a perfume that no other woman puts on. It is her personal Oblivion which she uses to revoke the perfume of the past and the perfume of other women in a man's memory, or a time that slipped by with a man.

What is required is a perfume that enables her to forget, but leaves others unable to forget her.

Men in the past, in the halcyon days of the desert, knew the scent of the women of the tribe, each and every one of them. They were able, in spite of veiled faces, to correctly identify a woman who was passing or who had just left a gathering from the fragrance she left behind. Perhaps we ought to try this trick to see to how individual our perfume is.

In your endeavour to forget a man, don't forget to change the perfume you wore for him. Give your friends the perfume of your previous emotional memory. Get rid of it so that you're not overcome by its bottles. Even in their silent presence, they ask you for him.

Your sticking to a perfume that you wore for him is an unspoken act of sticking by him; your acceptance of his taking possession of your senses even after you have separated from him.

You have to fall in love with a new perfume. This idea in itself will work magic on you. It will convince you that something has come to an end and that something else is coming. This will have the fragrance of a perfume that will cling to you from the first spray, exactly like the first sight.

Don't forget to prepare for choosing the perfume of your days to come by wearing your most beautiful clothes and finest accessories.

The occasion deserves you making yourself beautiful. You have a date with the perfume of a new love. Even if love doesn't come, you should concoct for absence a beautiful perfume to beautify your waiting.

The most wonderful perfume remains the one mixed by Guerlain and that bears his name. In the 1940s he invented a perfume for one woman for one night which he gave as a present to the woman he loved. (I used to think that in this way he gave her the only perfume for love, like a wedding dress tailor-made for one woman to wear on one occasion. Now I am tempted to ask whether he was giving her the perfume of forgetting?)

That is a perfume without promises, without a future, without commitments, a perfume without memory. Like Shahrazaad, its story comes to an end when the morning comes. Among its unadvertised features is that it does not linger in a man's memory and takes him back to the perfume of his first woman.

A heart in being drawn to you
betrays me
where you go, it follows
holding on to the hem of your perfume
—the Author

Foil his agents' conspiracy!

How strange! You're with me but still I yearn
and ask everyone I meet about you
You live inside my iris but my eyes still need you
You live within my ribs but my heart still needs you
—the Author

I confess. I wrote this book to fool around with forgetting. That is because we cannot have a serious debate with memory. It has weapons we are defenceless against.

Memory defeats us because it has a fifth column inside us that manages its affairs to the advantage of a lover and conspires against us to his benefit. All your senses are working as agents for him, some with thc rank of liaison officer.

Menachem Begin would say, 'For each five of Arafat's retinue, three are his and two are mine.'

When Israel had two agents for every five of Arafat's circle, it could decimate the Palestinian cause. In which case, what do you think if all five were agents, living inside you and working for the cause of a stranger who claims to be a lover? Israel wouldn't have won all those wars were it not for the abundance of collaborators and spies. Your senses hand your sweetheart victory over you. You discover this too late, as in all tales of espionage.

Only when you try to forget a man do the agents reveal themselves. You aren't in a war against one man, but against the combined forces of the KGB, CIA and Gestapo. He has left them to fight the war on his behalf inside you and gone AWOL.

They are lodged in your bone marrow, in your veins, in your retina, in your nostrils and in the pores of your skin.

What is the difference between lover and occupier then? Given that he has set up a settlement on the territory of your being.

He is your vision, your smell and your sight. He is the words you speak, and your silent ranting. He is your skin – can you shed your skin? He is your cells and pores. He is the demon of your insomnia and the deity of sleep. He is the poison you take throughout the day between meals. He is the meal you consume to remain alive.

Your five senses are conscripted round the clock in his defence. They demand you find him and bring him down from heaven or raise him from under the ground.

The greatest shock when you plunge into the battle to forget is the discovery that your senses have betrayed you. That it is up to you alone, if you so wish, to exorcise this emotional demon from your body. You will have to declare war on yourself. You will have to shout out 'No!' at the top of your voice to the sense that evokes his cologne, the sense that evokes his voice, the sense that evokes the taste of his kiss, the sense that evokes his touch, the sense that evokes his figure, his walk, his laugh, his way of sitting, his clothing.

You are, to put it briefly, entering a world war single-handed against the massed armies of the allies.

God help you, woman!

In spite of this, do not despair. Everyone you encounter in life has embarked on such battles and emerged victorious, more or less!

I longed for you, cursed be the night you departed

—Faisal al-Rashid

My memories, O my memories

WE FORGET NOTHING WE WISH TO FORGET.
WE FORGET EVERYTHING ELSE
—Bouri Sufyan

Forgetting a person whom you spent years loving does not imply that you have erased him from memory. You have merely changed his location. He is no longer at the front of your mind, present every day in all his details. He is no longer a memory all the time. Sometimes he is gone. Someone else is needed to take his place and push his presence to the bottom of the memory stack.

This is because memories do not die. They are in motion within, they fade to escape our efforts to kill them. Then at the first opportunity they're back and surface in our hearts. We welcome them like a visitor we haven't seen for ages who has come to say hi and then continue on his way.

Memories are vagrant. They can't be tied down however we tempt them to stay among us.

They leave as they came. No memories linger. When they visit, none are transformed into real life. Here lies the secret of our welcoming them, and our pain when they abandon us. They are what has been saved of a past life.

Nobody can claim that they control their memories, or that they do not need to seek them in corners behind cobwebs of time. They control us; they seek us out when they will.

My opinion is confirmed by psychoanalyst Patrick Estrade in his book *You Are What You Remember*. He writes, 'Memories are our inner skin. They form our personality without our knowledge. The memories we recall on particular occasions are the key to solving many of the problems which become our lives.'

In the author's opinion, memories do not live inside us, rather they envelop our lives. They are all the things around us that we surround ourselves with: what we touch, what we wear, what we keep, what has no use but we refuse to throw away. They are what ensnares us.

Memories are our other identity whose truth we conceal from others. The above author even came up with a new slogan, 'Tell me what you remember, and I'll tell you who you are', which is the truest psychological catchphrase I've come across. Give this game a try: get to know yourselves by asking: What exactly do you remember? Which memories have been saved from oblivion during your journey through life's labyrinth? Any memories which have not deserted you over the course of this life are the very ones that rule your life.

Forgetting . . . has the power and holds the key

—Maurice Blanchot

*Make your memories into tabbouleh**

IF YOUR WIFE'S HANDS ALWAYS SMELL OF ONIONS,
KNOW SHE IS PRACTISING WITH A KNIFE. PRAY WHY?!
—Proverb

We die minors without having attained the legal age for forgetting. There is nothing we can do against memory; it resides amidst fossilised emotions. Therefore some think that the solution lies in getting rid of memories when they strike, so that we do not give them the opportunity to penetrate and percolate inside us. Memories are only the accumulation of the present.

New Yorkers have come up with a novel way of discarding and ridding themselves of the previous year's memories that they wish to forget. On New Year's Eve they set up a giant shredder in Time Square into which they throw, with suitably festive spirit, all they wish to have no place in their lives afterwards.

A man throws away a photo of a girlfriend who cheated on him; another throws away his debts. A woman flings away her mobile phone; another the presents from an ex-lover. Women make speeches and swear oaths to forget while men curse, laugh and applaud.

After midnight on New Year, ugly memories have been dumped into a rubbish pit. People head home happy after having shed the memories that make their lives miserable.

* Lebanese salad based on bulgar wheat, tomatoes and parsley.

You do not need to wait for New Year's Eve to cast your unhappiness into the memory shredder. You're not short of occasions: it might be the anniversary of when you first met, the passage of a year's worth of his silence and cold shouldering, the anniversary of the last time you were together, or the memorial of his mortal blow and your going into mourning.

In the absence of a 'shredder', enter the kitchen of love and shred everything that has become a source of irritation and pain in your life. Turn the pulp of memories into tabbouleh. Rehydrate the bulgur wheat of your hopes that have desiccated in his absence. Chop up a delicious organic wild tomato. Use the sharpest knife to mince the past in one go: so you don't fall into the trap of repeating it.

Of course you can't acquire forgetting for the price of a bunch of parsley. What matters, however, isn't the parsley but the knife. What's important is to crush the memories that crush you without mercy every day.

I also advise you to open the fridge of the past. Discard everything in it that's gone rotten without you noticing, everything past its use by date and not worth keeping. Throw away the half-opened packets of wishes whose surface is covered in mould, the sorrows as soft as camembert, imported from a country that no longer exports delicacies to the tables of your love, and which will only give the rats more of an appetite to visit you.

The greens that remain in the fridge of your memories, cook with couscous. Invite your girlfriends for dinner without telling them the occasion. Adorn the table of forgetting with candlesticks. Be happy as you contemplate the candles melting away. You were like that before today.

The shredder has rescued you from the self-immolation of the past. It's okay if you cried on your own at the end of the evening.

'Whenever a tear is shed, a candle is lit,' according to the Algerian proverb.

Women buffeted by forgetting

I swear I never betrayed you
never did I suspect my heart
had the strength to live after you
but disappointment has taught me
to get by without you
I just forget to stay awake for you
I just refuse to weep for you
I'm simply too distracted to remember you
the greatest betrayal is to forget

—the Author

We had a date
in a new neighbourhood for us
we sat around a rectangular table
for the first time
we cast an eye over the menu
and over the list of drinks
without casting an eye at each other
instead of tea we ordered a cup of forgetting
and as main course a whole load of lies.

We added a little ice to our glass of love
we added a little refinement to our words
we put our madness in our pockets
and our longing in our handbag
we wore outfits that have no memory
and hung up the past with our coats on the rack
so love passed us by without recognising us [. . .]

When the table of cravings is cleared
how ridiculous it seems to continue to sit at it
and how stupid the lovers seem
so why stay? All of this lying is too much to bear
clear your table, love
it's time for this heart to walk away.

The Author, from 'It's Time for this Heart to Walk Away', 1986

That telephone creature who's messing with your life

She has no age
she reaches adulthood with a kiss
and enters menopause
when the phone stops ringing
God help the woman
who meets love on your lips
—the Author

Warning:

I hope you will not skip this chapter because you will undoubtedly need to refer back to it as long as you live. As long as you don't want to die in an incident of openly declared silence at the hands of a man who has, all of a sudden, decided to kill you by means of a telephonically-induced seizure. This is after he has spent months, maybe years, trying to make you addicted and clinically dependent to his voice.

Women are unanimous that things usually begin like this: a man who seems mildly phone obsessive invades your life telephonically, and you can't tell to what extent he's sane or mad. He phones you as many times as there are hours in the day. He sends you a text wherever he goes to tell you something of such importance it cannot be delayed: that he needs you at every moment.

'I'm not home, I'm in your heart.'

'I'm stuck in traffic and I'm stuck on you.'

'I'm going home, to you.'

'I'm buying bread. But my only sustenance is you.'

'I'm having dinner with friends, but I'm only hungry for you.'

'I'll sleep forever, if it's in your eyes.'

'Good morning. You are all my mornings.'

The days pass in this way and you keep him company, at daybreak and twilight, wherever he is and whatever he does, down to every last detail, as though you were a subscriber to a twenty-four-hour breaking-news service.

Because he calls you all the time, it might happen that your phone is engaged. Here is born the nucleus of the problem out of which others will multiply, you know not how, in the face of your incredulity.

This lover, who by virtue of distance has been transformed into a telephone creature, will see your phone's being busy as meaning your being too busy for him and, perhaps, your cheating on him. The phone is 'his phone', and you are not supposed to have any other job than him, even if you are editor of a global news channel.

A girlfriend asks me on the verge of tears, 'What do I do? Problems have started between us. Whenever he finds my phone engaged, it's Judgement Day, and he stops calling me for a day or two.' I give her the good news: 'One day he'll stop for days, then weeks and perhaps longer.' She wails, 'But I love him. You know how much I love him. There's no one else in my life. He's the love of my life and I don't want to lose him.'

But, my dear, from the moment the maggot of doubt entered his heart, you've come under threat of losing him. He will believe the maggot and not believe you.

(Before this book went to press, my prediction came true and this friend lost the love of her life.)

Lovers were happier and more confident and trusting of each other before Alexander Grahame Bell came along – God damn him –

and invented the telephone. It is a sufficient curse for him that he was unable to phone, not even once, his mother or his wife, because they were both deaf.

In vain I explain to my friend that in the same way as revolutions consume their children the telephone consumes its lovers. It is the means of their own demise. I tell her that she has to prepare from now on to cut the telephonic umbilical cord which joins her to that man night and day.

During the dinner party, her eyes filled with tears because another friend, a star of the Gulf media, maybe even its biggest star, seconded my opinion. She gave me a start when she confessed that, for three years, she had lived outside the galaxy of love for the same reason. We shouted in amazement, 'You haven't loved anyone since?' She said, 'No. He was the love of my life.'

For his part, he didn't believe that a woman of such beauty, celebrity and popularity would be faithful to him. The maggot insinuated to him, 'How could she be faithful to you when she is surrounded by such crowds of the rich and famous!' The really painful thing is that he didn't know she was still devoted to him. Would he be happy or sad at all the waste? And how do you think he interpreted her decision not to call him ever again once he suddenly stopped calling? Perhaps he thought she was busy with another love affair, and that her phone like her heart was out of service and going along with the split and the betrayal.

The other friend comforted her: 'Don't be sad. I promise you that it's not a more beautiful or popular woman that has taken your place. He's looking for security with a woman who's mediocre in everything. A man usually looks for an ordinary woman to be his refuge. He doesn't want a great love, but a woman who gives him a sense of greatness.'

The poor woman replied: 'What about beautiful successful woman then? Whom do they have?'

'They have successful self-confident men,' answered the other friend.

I went away from the dinner party under an emotional black cloud. I do not understand how misunderstanding, mistrust and misfortune make a combined effort to destroy all these beautiful love affairs without the other half being aware of how wicked and abusive he is in blowing hot and cold on the phone.

The hearts of women die because a man, without the slightest sense of guilt, storms into their lives and then cruelly and without explanation abandons them and goes on to amuse himself crushing the heart of another woman to whom he has run away from the first, and so viciously on.

Is it the superabundance of speech between lovers that kills love? The superabundance of detail which love needs to survive, but not to dream?

Love needs intrigue, little secrets for which the telephone pathology leaves no room. Thus a couple's love becomes stronger, more violent, after the phoning stops. This forces each of them to create a hypothetical life for the other on the basis of what they know from old habits and secrets. Love, in spite of the pain, turns beautiful as in olden times. Only in the grand emotions of the great lovers does a split not kill but revive. It inflames love and provides it with the fuel it needs: the defiance of fate by loyalty to a person even though you do not know what he is doing on the other side of life. His familiar habits and what he said to you over the months and years have given you confidence in who he really is.

Nevertheless, you will be plagued by misgivings and suspicions in the face of his silence. For silence is the playground of emotional ambiguity. Over time you will doubt every token, even the female voice of the automated message that answers you.

'I hate the woman who says, "The number your have dialled is currently unavailable." How can I be sure she isn't one of those women around you!' says Marie al-Qusaifi.

A rise in the telephone bill is not definite proof
of a rise in the value of the words spoken.
—the Author

That love-killing pride

LOVE REACHES ITS PEAK WHEN THE WOMAN GIVES UP HER STUBBORNNESS AND THE MAN HIS PRIDE

—Honoré de Balzac

Don't contest with a man by offering him more concessions. When shopping, a man doesn't like sales; it's the same with love: he wants what's rare and expensive.

One day, for sure, he will test your capacity for patience with a separation that might be final. His disappearance may last for days, weeks or months or be the end that you're still unaware of.

So be it. Enter the arena of his silence. You will grow with your patience towards him. Enjoy the break. Don't live in torment; take the separation as training in pride and self-assertion. 'The only thing stronger than love is the pride of unassailable women,' the saying goes.

Over time, you will stop counting the days you have not heard his voice, the special occasions and holidays that he intentionally let slip past, despite his having sent greetings to people who mean far less to him than you.

This will not be easy. But his desertion is the fuel of your defiance, so increase it as much as you can. You have to acquire new habits to slay the old ones. Before all of this, you have to nourish your sense of superiority in the confrontation with the one who was your closest soul mate but has turned into your archenemy. This is because he holds your keys and knows the unguarded entrances to your heart. He knows how weak you are towards him.

Don't weaken and dial his number. You will lose your self-esteem but you won't win *him* back.

Particularly through the efforts to outdo each other in pride, big love dies the cheapest death. It dies for the sake of two foolish lovers, enflamed with passion and in misery at the same time, who try to boost their chances of winning a contest in being harsh unto death. 'We're all numbers, my dear. Let's leave life to add us together, before death subtracts us into dust.'

I know of no greater crime against ourselves and against love, and of no loss more egregious and foolish.

But as long as this is the criminal game which men find pleasurable to play, we have no choice but to descend into the arena and win the round, even if this requires us to cauterise our hearts as a last resort.

I have a girlfriend who was betrayed by her own hand when she was overwhelmed by longing. Weeks after breaking up with the man she loved, she dialled his number. When he hung up on her, she lit a cigarette and used it to burn her right hand, so that whenever she saw the scar, she would hate him, and her hand would refuse to dial again.

He went to extremes in rejecting her, because he believed that, as was his custom, he could badly mistreat her and still find her waiting for him when he came back. He never for a moment imagined that this time she wouldn't be waiting. A man had come into her life who crowned her a princess and loved and pampered her as no man had. He adored her to the extent of kissing her toes, and never noticed the traces of the burn on her hand.

Her latest news was that the first lover had come from abroad to say goodbye: he was about to die. An illness had struck him out of the blue in his prime and all his pride, and his health had deteriorated. He told her that he had not forgotten her one day in four years, and that he loved only her.

My friend had not stopped crying and did not know what to do. She called me and said, 'I've got a story for you that you must write.

You remember so-and-so. Well he's come back.' I shouted, 'No! You're joking!' She said, 'He came to say goodbye to me.' I said, 'Didn't you split up years ago?' She said, 'He's saying goodbye to me this time because he might die.'

When he married another woman in his own country, he hadn't said goodbye. I had seen her cry in all the countries we travelled to together: whenever she saw a woman on the phone to her lover; whenever she heard a song from his country; whenever two people got married.

My girlfriend, who years ago cried on account of his abuse and abandonment, had, in the flush of her new love, reverted to crying for him. She proposed that she live with him for the rest of his life and keep him company touring the world's hospitals. She swore to him that by the miracle of her love she would be able to cure him. But he replied that he wanted her as a wife not a nurse and left for his fate.

His sense that there was another love in her life made his illness worse. She had tried to conceal it from him so as not to increase his pain.

There are two kinds of misery: the first is not getting what you want; the second is to get it, but too late, when you have changed and what you want has changed (after you've been made miserable for several years).

I'm still asking myself: who's wrong and who's more wronged in this tale?

Perhaps fate, which has all the answers, answered that her lover was the most wrong to himself and her. He thought he could transgress a true love and build married life on its ruins. But in the face of death and at a moment of true honesty, the voice of the heart spoke up and asked for the wife of his heart. He discovered that it's a crime to die far from our hearts.

Why then was he stubborn all those years?

Why did he make them both miserable?

Why did he cry in secret, and make her cry?

Why did he, a Bedouin jealous like the Arabian gazelle, leave her to another man?

What's most likely is that the possibility of losing her did not enter his calculations. Men believe women are essentially there to wait for them, and that they are too weak to make up their minds to leave or stick to the decision. But there is a point at which loyalty becomes self-abasement.

I testify that she was faithful to him even after the separation. She was faithful like a modern woman who fell in love with a tribal elder. He wasn't an elder: he was a man who loved like a Bedouin. He did not anticipate how much a woman could give, how much she could wait, until along came fate one day and presented her with a love to make her forget her misery.

When relinquishing the love of his life, man, out of pride, believes he will emerge triumphant. The acceptance of egregious losses, merely out of defiance and for no other reason, is part of the virility of our Arab history, where the despotic ruler, out of stubbornness, sacrifices his nation and hands it to the occupier so as not to lose face and back down.

At his moment of weakness before love, man refuses to return, apologetic and broken, to his great love. After a split, his upbringing prevents him from seeing the absolutely most beautiful moments of his life.

This is a love that could have risen from its ashes, from the absence and the wounds, more beautiful and more mature.

More than once he wanted to dial her number. What he didn't expect was that she would gasp at the other end of the line and give him more love than he dreamt of. Women adore those who come back to them to say, 'I cannot live without you.' Actually, women only despise tyrants and emotional cowards.

Nevertheless, a man too preoccupied to love and who lords it over his lover does not discover until it is too late the truth of the advice that a Swedish family rights organisation made into its motto: 'You won't have regrets on your deathbed because you didn't get a promotion, but because you didn't spend enough time with the ones you love.'

He took everything into account except death.

Death, in whose presence all falsehood dies and all emotional outbidding comes to an end. There is no pride before it for the great. It is the one truth before which everyone is insignificant.

The moment death makes an appearance, does a man have any voice left to say to a woman, divided from him by continents of separation and defiance, that he loved her unto death?

What is even more painful is if she dies before him and leaves him to spend the rest of his life bleeding with regret because, from now on, he doesn't know what to do with all the words he didn't say to her and which will expire with him, if they don't kill him.

My friend still relives her story in tears whenever she calls me. Confronted with this, I thought that quarrelling lovers, vying to outdo each other in causing harm with all the fierceness and might of life, ought to pause, even if for only one day during the months and years of the split, to think about the possibility of the other's death.

They should call to mind the dead body of their beloved, lifeless and cold, before they commit it to the ground. To mourn for them when they are alive, so as not to mourn for them dead. Then time will have run out for ever, and they will no longer have the eyes to see the tears shed for them. When their mortal blows no longer cause any pain to the body, the pain will become the lot of the one gripping the dagger.

How many love stories might have been saved if only the lovers had thought with the logic of death and not the logic of life.

Will lovers ever learn?

When I try to know if I have loved a person,
I imagine them dead and observe my body's reaction
—Broadcaster Amy Jenkins

Oppressor, thy day shall come

YOUR EYE SLEEPS BUT THE OPPRESSED ARE VIGILANT
PRAYING FOR YOUR DOWNFALL; GOD NEVER SHUTS HIS EYE
—the Author

Al-Asma'i related that he saw a man called Abu Sa'ib of Bani Makhzom clinging on to the cloth that covers the Kaaba whilst praying, 'O Lord God, take mercy on lovers, and take pity on the hearts of the beloved, in compassion and mercy, O Most Merciful.'

Al-Asma'i said, 'Abu Sa'ib, in such a place you would say such?'

He replied. 'Fie on thee! Petition for them is worth more than the Lesser Pilgrimage.' Then he recited:

Desertion, stay away from love and leave it
  to the lovers be sweet, O desertion
What do you wish from those whose eyelids
  are blistered and whose chests are afire
The traces of tears on their cheeks
  sparkling as if a deluge of raindrops
Slain on the bridge of love in their misery
  Fate toys with them

I read this tale after I had performed the Lesser Pilgrimage, a year

* A square stone building in the centre of the Great Mosque in Mecca.

before writing this. If I had known then that it was permissible for lovers to raise their complaints with God and, in His house, invoke evil on someone, as they invoke blessings on another, I would have taken advantage of my pilgrimage to settle scores. My companions would say to me, 'Be demanding, ask for what you want. Ask God for everything that comes to mind.' I would see those circling the Kaaba* repeating prayers, but not know what to request from God other than forgiveness, health and wellbeing for myself and all Muslims. I have always been embarrassed to ask God for anything related to everyday life. My thinking was that God knows what I want, and if he wished to, He would give it to me without me having to barter my prayers and fasting in exchange. That was until I read that God does not like those who do not ask and considers such behaviour arrogant and deserving of punishment.

Oops! This called for a rethink, and maybe a repeat pilgrimage.

The next time I shall, God willing, make practical preparations. I will have with me a clearly written and exhaustive list of names written in two colours: blue for those I am going to pray for, and red for those I am going to imprecate against. This is to stop the names getting jumbled in my head when I'm in the presence of God. My worries got worse when a woman told me that prayers may be misdirected in the heavenly sorting-office if they do not meet the conditions of prayer. These include the prayer being appended with the name of the mother of the person you are praying for, or imprecating against. Someone else said, 'No, the father's name is more important. A Muslim is called forward on the Day of Judgement by his father's name.'

Just imagine all those prayers with unspecified recipients. How in God's name will they find their way to Heaven?

I find it difficult to believe that you could be praying for Mohammed in Algeria, and your prayers go to a different Mohammed in Pakistan. You are imprecating against Abdullah, yet you don't know which one of the millions, from Malaysia to Somalia, bearing the same name will be struck by the curse.

In this case, the rarer the name, the lesser the likelihood of the prayer ending up with someone other than the intended recipient.

I would be happy if this were the case, because the personal name Ahlem is restricted to myself and the Emirati singer Ahlem.

Prayers, then, would not stray beyond the confines of the pair of us. On this basis, I found myself taking an interest in her. I started to suspect that many prayers meant for me, and which I have endeavoured to amass over my lifetime, have ended up at her door. This is due to her wealth, may God protect it, which, she has announced on more than one occasion, verges on one billion dollars. There is a light year of zeros between us. And this is despite her taking up singing professionally only fifteen years ago, while I have been writing for thirty! Perhaps bad luck haunts authors.

Given that prayer is the best guarantee against adversity, the situation mandates an initiative on her part to redistribute prosperity between us.

If she rejects the proposal, I will ask her to publicise her mother's name, so that I do not accidentally receive the imprecations of those she has crossed during her artistic career. Specially as the confusion between us grew when she was awarded an honorary doctorate. Imagine someone who wanted to be doubly certain about his prayers specifying that they meant 'Dr Ahlem PhD' personally, and this prayer also accruing to my lot.

This has caused me to ponder giving up the title which I spent five years in the corridors of the Sorbonne to acquire, and which I have not used in a single circumstance of my life. I cannot, however, renounce my name which, in my case, is real. This is an additional reason why prayers against her end up going to me!

But the whole matter is more complicated than it seems. If you wish to imprecate against the man who tormented you, made you cry and exacted your life or your eye, as the Egyptians say (meaning to give you a really hard time), then you need to be armed with his mother's name. On my life, this will be the mother of all battles and a mother of a difficulty. How can you ask a man for his mother's name if she's not your mother-in-law, or prospective mother-in-law?

Here it's a question of every woman's intelligence for itself, and the stupidity of the man out of whom she has to twist the name before he throttles her.

In this respect, I have no stratagem to give you. I still haven't quite taken it seriously. But being a novelist, I may one day return and suggest some scenarios for the task.

All your feminine wiles will be assessed by this exam.

One girlfriend advises you to ask him directly for his mother's name in the first few days of your acquaintance. At this early point, his happiness with a new love will make him ready to divulge anything. Included in this are any military secrets he may have been entrusted with and whose revelation threatens national security.

Another piece of advice from the same friend: write the name down straightaway in a notebook, in preparation for the day when you declare forgetting against him and forget, among everything you forget in the campaign to 'wipe your memory', his mother's name. This at the time when you need it most, to imprecate against him.

I know that men are right now reading these pages and saying, 'Have you seen how wicked women are? Is it reasonable that this sweet, kind woman who loved us is now beseeching God for Him to destroy us?'

My answer to them (in the King's English): Certainly, indeed, yes my good man.

It's injustice that pushes a woman to act out of character. And this has no connection with our being women. I have heard men praying the prayers of the oppressed against their lovers. There are also some women who are unfair, bullying and treacherous.

The issue here is related to our being women in love.

The matter ought to inspire confidence in men. A woman who imprecates curses upon you still loves you. While a woman praying for you at times and praying against you at times means that she still hasn't completely lost hope of you coming back. She is also afraid that God might really answer her prayers. Then she would go mad and be the first to die of sorrow for you.

Thus, among God's blessings to us is that He does not answer lovers' prayers, because they are basically confused and do not know what exactly they want. We have in Bothaina's Jameel, the imam of lovers, a perfect example of the swinging opinions of lovers and their contradictory requests and prayers for being together and being apart.

He is called by his lover's name the Jameel of Bothaina because of his extraordinary passion for her. He once said:

'If my leg were paralysed and its cure
were the beloved's prayer, you would be my prayer.'

It came to pass that Jameel, from the anguish of abandonment, lost his mind and imprecated Bothaina with blindness. This curse seems to have universal application to men from antiquity to the present day. Twenty years ago, I heard a man in Algeria praying against a relation of mine who had refused to marry him as follows, 'May God blind you, and you not find a guide.'

As for Bothaina's Jameel, he once again met his beloved after their long estrangement. They recriminated together for an hour then she said to him, 'Darn it Jameel. You claim to love me truly, but didn't you say:

"May God cast sand into Bothaina's eyes
and canker into the gaps between her teeth!"'

He remained silent a long while in tears. Then he said, 'But I am the one who said:

"Would that I were blind and deaf, led by
Bothaina, her speech not concealed from me."'

She replied: 'What has made you choose such perdition? Is there not enough good health to suffice us?'

How do you expect God to respond to the prayer of a lover for his beloved to go blind who then regrets the horror of what he's asked for and tearfully prays again that he be blinded instead, and she be his guide.

Imagine for a moment if God were to answer his prayer on both occasions. Wouldn't both of them have been blinded?

I know that all these arguments will not dissuade some readers from imprecating against their lovers or their faithless husbands. Nothing will extinguish the fire that consumes them except tears in the presence of God, when they give vent to their complaints against the abuse of those they loved and were faithful to but who deserted them.

To them I say, rejoice, for 'The one who oppresses will find God his enemy.'

When the oppression is real and the pain and injustice great, God, may He be praised, must avenge you from those who beguiled you. He is the Best Beguiler. [Quran 3:54]

To readers in pain who are seeking solace and forgetfulness, I offer these prayers which I collected for you from my friends, and some that are my own.

Now clever ones, if you have managed to obtain his mother's name, you must choose the appropriate occasion to offer it up to Heaven. If you've missed the month of Ramadan, its last ten days and Laylat al-Qadr*, then you have the dawn prayer. For no prayer is rebuffed from one standing in God's presence at that time of day. Pray

* Laylat al-Qadr is the anniversary of the night in which the Quran is said to have been revealed.

the set prayer, then cry with the passion of a forsaken woman and pick one from the prayers below:

The prayer of the pious woman

O Lord God, make him forgotten to oblivion. O Lord God, wipe him from my heart as Thou wiped sadness from the heart of Mohammed.

The prayer of the abused woman

Vengeance, O Lord, the Avenger, for every moment of truth when I was honestly true to him, and he rewarded me with deceit and desertion. May it be returned to him, God willing, as terrible pain.

The prayer of the God-fearing woman

O Lord God, You are his adversary. I entrust the business of him to You. Let me bear witness to Your tyranny, for he was, O Lord, a tyrant.

The prayer of the subordinate woman

If one of them embitters you with his hurtfulness, accuses you of something you have nothing to do with, does you down in public and spread lies about you, you may pray, 'O Lord God, I gave my honour as his alms, but Thou knowest me better, so be my agent against him.'

The prayer of the deranged woman

O Lord God, lodge of every complaint, hearer of every secret, witness of every trial, by the glory of Mohammed return him to me just as he was, with his afflictions and hardships, his jealousy, suspicions and bouts of rage.

Keep me his slave, prisoner of his ribcage. Fill my phone with his messages, and my days with his interrogations and questions. Turn me from all occupations but him, all ambitions but his. Make my time pass in pampering him, my days in adorning him and boosting him among men. Keep the insinuations in his heart and multiply his jealousy over me and madness for me.

I am content, from You, O God, with all my destined hardships to come. For there is no hardship more lethal to me than his desertion. My want was severe in his absence, my strength was diminished, my activity weakened and my memory awakened.

I plead with You, O God, the plea of the deranged thwarted woman, who has lost her mind since he left. There is none who can deliver her but You, O Most Merciful.

There is no God but You, may You be praised, I have been one of the wrongdoers.

The prayer of the wise woman (very wise)

O Lord God, make the most beautiful of my days the day he falls in love with the first woman who encounters him. And make the most beautiful day of his life the day I fall in love with a man whose character matches my dignity.

The prayer of the wicked woman

(I heard this prayer ten years ago from a Lebanese friend who used it against a man she had loved): 'God strike him with paralysis and extend his life.'

The prayer of the deceived woman

(A prayer I heard in Morocco to frustrate a man's sexual performance): 'Lord, make him cotton and the women concrete.'

This is a most terrible and cunning invocation. How can a thread penetrate a wall! The aim of this prayer is for the man to be made impotent with every woman to the point of being ashamed of himself.

The mother of prayers

You will ask me: which is your prayer?

My prayer, my dears, appears a blessing but masks a curse:

O Lord God, give him a double helping of all he gave me.

This is my prayer against all those who have been unfair to me. I know of no prayer more just and more cunning at the same time, in your sure knowledge of how great his evil was compared with his kindness, and his betrayal compared to his goodness.

You can now sleep forevermore with confidence. It's better to sleep oppressed than to sleep an oppressor.

Important notice:

There is one prayer among those above that I wash my hands of and, out of responsibility, warn you against raising, particularly during the last ten days of Ramadan or at dawn, for if God answers, it will turn against you.

It's left to you to find out, 'without asking a friend!' (as Chris Tarrant would say).

Beware the prayer of the oppressed man,
for there is no barrier between him and God
—Hadith

Remember the night of the goat-kid

NOT PAIN
BUT ITS SITE AFTER IT FADES
ITS OWN SITE
REMAINS TENDER
AT THE STING OF WHAT FADES
—Bassam Hajjar

There is a Bedouin cautionary tale that my mother enjoys telling.

Once there was a woman of one of the Bedouin tribes of the Algerian south whose daughter had married and moved to live under the protection of another tribe. She went to visit her daughter who was overjoyed to see her mother and slaughtered a goat-kid in her honour.

When her husband came home in the evening, before he entered the tent he went to check on his flocks. He found the tally short by one goat. He went in to his wife and found her preparing the evening meal. He then proceeded to beat her furiously because she had slaughtered the goat.

Despondent, the mother pretended to sleep and did not eat the evening meal. Before dawn she departed back to her tribe. After some time a messenger between the two tribes came and told her that her daughter's husband had died.

The mother went to visit her daughter and found her on the ground tearing at her hair and covering herself with dust in mourning and grief for her husband. 'She wished she were like him, covered with dust.'

Upon seeing her in this state, her mother said to her, 'Weep, weep, indulge in weeping. Then remember the night of the goat-kid.' The daughter then remembered how much she had cried at the hands of her husband the night of the goat-kid when he had angrily and unjustly beaten her. She stopped crying, got to her feet and brushed off the dust. Her story has become proverbial among women since then.

Before you bewail a man, slap yourself and rend your clothing, remember the 'night of the goat-kid'. Remember those bruises whose black-and-blue tinged your heart, the pain and the insults that love forgave and concealed, but that today memory lays bare after love has lifted their immunity.

A journalist friend remained obsessed with the love of a man. For three years she described him to me as if he were Ibn Zaydun in his legendary love for Walada bint al-Mustakfi. He was the greatest, the most honest, a king among men. But in his moments of rage he would say hurtful things to her. She has only confessed them to me now, years later, because she is only able to say them now. Once he said to her, 'You're one big lie. So you think you're a big-shot journalist, but there are a million women more important and more beautiful than you. So-and-so for example has a million times more honour than you. How she wishes I would just say hello to her, and I don't.'

Years passed and my friend could not forget that the man she loved had assessed her worth against a woman who was her inferior in achievement and morals.

This So-and-so was a journalist ready to sell herself in return for a conference abroad. She was only interested in being everywhere so she might attain some celebrity. Whereas my friend was unwilling to knock on the doors of the media organisations. She refused to compromise her dignity in return for a reward, however valuable.

As a result she stopped working for a while so as not to give him reason to be jealous. Her only occupation was pampering this man for whom she had given up everything on the chance he would trust her and marry her. Even so he didn't come to trust her, and didn't care about the opportunities he had caused her to lose. One of the nights of the goat-kid he beat her up with all his machismo, after fancying that he had seen her smiling over dinner . . . at the waiter!

I asked her in astonishment, 'How did you stay with a man like that?'

She answered, 'He had his good points, unusual qualities that made me forget his faults. He was tender, constant, honourable and giving. But he was aggressively jealous, plagued by doubts and foul-mouthed. His fits of rage had no logic and were unbearable. When I remember them even now I'm reduced to tears as though I were reliving them.'

This is because pain awakens belatedly and endures long after the beautiful memories.

The pain is another's mistreatment and victimisation of you. His not believing your solemn promise, doubting your truthfulness, cheapening your tears.

Then one day you say, 'Enough!'

It's not possible for such mistreatment to be love. You will slam the door behind you and leave. To leave him to the millions of women he thought 'more important', 'more honourable', 'more beautiful', 'more honest' and 'more whatever'. He's now theirs. The matter no longer concerns you.

My friend packed her bags and went to work at the UN in New York. She didn't take tears or regrets with her. She took the story of the night of the goat-kid.

The eye deceives itself when it loves.
The ear believes another when it hates
—Proverb

Less talk

THE PERSON WHO WANTS TO SURVIVE OUGHT TO SAY HALF THE TRUTH AND HIDE HALF THEIR FEELINGS
—Jean Cocteau

The problem consists of a few words that when you fall under their sway become thousands.

They are a burning fuse that can be snuffed out by tolerance or a word of apology from the one in the wrong. One half of a couple conceding his or her pride or right should not be deemed a loss. Rather it is a wonderful act of sacrifice that will add to his or her esteem in the eyes of the lover and will rescue love from the jaws of defiance.

However, this 'fuse of a problem' may, out of stubbornness, turn into an out-of-control blaze when it is stoked by the fuel of cruel words that each one has been storing up in their heart for just such a day.

Arguments in relationships spiral because in each argument we do not confront the new and unforeseen problem that crops up, rather, we fall back on a list of past grievances which the man (for the most part) runs through on every occasion. This is an itemised list within the inventory of complaints and indictments that he has collected over the course of the relationship since the day you met until judgement day. To this is appended all the emotional services he rendered the day he forgave you your sins, most of which were committed out of love for him.

He does this in the fashion of Fidel Castro, some of whose speeches lasted for seven hours on account of his insistence on always reminding the Cuban people of everything he had achieved for them, and all the luxury he had bestowed on them during over half a century of rule. These speeches went on for so long that healthy members of the wretched audience fell ill and the already sick died, women fell pregnant and those whose contractions began gave birth during the thunderous speech. It even happened once that the beloved, divine Comandante himself slipped into unconsciousness due to a plethora of words.

Don't allow words to assassinate lovers, when one word is enough to save love.

Practical Advice:

There are men who do not know that words are like bullets and cannot be taken back. At a moment of rage he will empty the magazine of words into you. The hurt will come as a shock. You didn't anticipate this lover could bear such a quantity of evil and malice inside.

Anger reveals a man's true character. A wise man once gave this piece of advice, 'One who has got angry with you three times and not said anything wicked about you, choose as your friend.'

Beware a man who is quick to anger and finds it hard to control his outbursts. Whatever his character, and perhaps he has innumerable virtues, has a good heart and is a rare lover, one fit of rage, when his mouth spews lava and fire at you, will turn your heart into a city laid waste (like Chernobyl) to whose lungs it will be hard to restore a pure life.

A man who did not know how to respond
to a kiss
I left in lipstick
on his mirror
wrote with a cut-throat razor
on my heart:
'I love you'
—the Author

The destruction of what was once beautiful

In the way you've destroyed your life here,
in this little corner, you've destroyed it everywhere else
—Cavafy

He invited me to have tea with him when he was passing through Beirut. Uncharacteristically, I accepted the invitation. I thought maybe he needed me as an envoy to my friend whom he had split up with months before.

He said, while lighting his third cigarette, 'I'm over her and I'm going to fall in love.' Then he reiterated in a loud voice, 'I'm going to fall in love!'

I did not tell him that premeditated love is not love, nor that a man whose design is love does not need to announce this in a loud voice nor relay it to someone he's got over.

His gaunt and tired features did not go with what he was saying. The person he claimed to have gotten over had infected him as he had infected her. Their love, like a malignant disease, had in its final stages ravaged everything.

A man wrecked by doubts was sitting in front of me. His suspicions had no logical basis but he was insistent on them. He needed to be the victim to recover. Convincing him of the opposite would have upset his balance and destroyed the case on which he based his defence and which he tirelessly repeated.

He sought me so I could bear witness to the ruins of a grand passion. A man whom I knew as refined and gallant was now taking random pot shots at the one he loved. He suggested I look over her text messages to him.

I said, 'This woman wished to die before you, so that she wouldn't be left without you. How could you leave her alive and give up on her?'

He answered, 'You've been deceived by her, like I was.'

Hopeless. He had been jealous of the very clothes she wore, and was now saying that his greatest happiness would be hearing she was happy with another man.

This wasn't funny. It was a joke emerging from the depths of pain and despondency.

He must have suffered so much to say such a thing. But my friend had suffered as much. She had given everything and kept nothing for herself, because she never expected this to happen.

She had waited for him such a long time. Whenever I tempted her to end her torment and open her heart to another, she said, 'After him there's only the grave.'

He didn't believe a word I was saying about her.

I defended the legend of their love as best I could, but the pain had blinded him. He could not hear any voice apart from the insinuating voice of his jealousy.

I asked him, 'I want you to tell me exactly what she did that day for you to make up your mind to leave her.'

He responded nervously, 'Ask her. She knows the reason.'

An ambiguous silence prevailed.

He claimed to have doubts about her, I incline to doubts about him. A man who offers no evidence of what he says is a liar, or in the most charitable interpretation has gone so far in his imaginings and suspicion as to turn his nightmares into a reality he perceives with his own eyes.

'But she doesn't know. That's exactly what's making her miserable.'

He once again sought protection in his vagueness, repeating, 'But she does know.'

There's nothing more dejecting than your lover being hostile to you without explanation; nothing more painful than being dumped for no reason, and being told whenever you ask that you know the reason. This isn't only the height of injustice and abuse, but also the height of cowardice. Did the decision to leave require the disguise of a lie that would allow him to deny her?

I thought that, in spite of this, he had yet to touch the depths of his pain. He would reach this years later when the love between them had died. He might by then have loved another woman, and she loved another man, and they would meet by chance in the twilight of life, when the fires between them had long gone out.

Only on that day, when she tells him the details of her mourning and her loyalty, will he believe her, and the rusty dagger of regret stab him. How had he abandoned her in her despair at him and let her go to another man.

When we parted ways his ruin spread to my heart. I feared for love from what I saw. I feared for every love in the present and in the future. And I was sad in advance for all the lovers in the world.

If such a stronghold of love could end in this way, then bid the world goodbye. What is the point then in writing about love?

They believed that their love was even stronger than death. But a lover stronger than death is not stronger than a tiny insect, the invisible maggot of doubt, that with its whisperings eats away the tree of love from the inside and will one day make it in all its majesty fall to the ground, despite the lushness of its leaves.

We parted. I saw him move away with long strides like a man speeding towards some fate.

The man shod in his forgetting
forgot to tie the laces
certainly
he will trip over memories
—the Author

Keep yourself beautiful with the memory of how it began

I BUILT SUCH ALLURING CASTLES THAT THEIR RUINS NOW SUFFICE

—Popular saying

I had to deliver the death notice to my friend.

How would I tell her that she was now out of the life of the man for whom she'd put her life on hold. Why hadn't he let her know his decision months ago? His intention was undoubtedly to waste more of her time. While he was getting over her, she was waiting for him and getting more lovesick each day.

I was worried she might collapse on hearing the news, for she had been confident of his return; the return of the beautiful fervour that had blazed between them and lit up the world. No matter what happened some sparks would remain scattered in the heart ready to reignite the flames of longing. But he wanted to make her feel that everything between them, including the beautiful memories, had gone out.

The story of my brother Yaseen's car crash occurred to me. In a terrifying accident he had smashed up my sister's new car when he had been driving it on a visit to Algeria. He only came out alive by a miracle.

With a view to her reaction, he said to her while on his way home that day, 'I've got some good news and some bad news for you. Which do you want first?'

Sophia replied in astonishment, 'The good news.'

He said, 'You've gained a brother. I was resurrected today.'

She hurriedly asked, 'And the bad news?'

He said, 'You've lost a car. I totally wrote it off.'

When Sophia saw the state of the car that Yaseen had emerged from alive, she forgot her material loss in spite of its extent. For days, whenever she saw Yaseen she thanked God he had survived.

I went to my friend and found her avidly awaiting my report on the meeting. I said to her over coffee, 'I've got some good news and some bad news for you. Which do you want first?'

She said in consternation, 'The good news.'

I said, 'Rejoice for you've gained yourself.'

She hurriedly asked, 'And the bad news?'

I said, 'You've lost that man.'

She put the coffee cup back on the table and tears sparkled in her eyes.

I said, 'Don't be sad. There's nothing anymore that can save him. He doesn't even resemble himself anymore.'

'But the likes of him don't change.'

'When doubts take over someone, they change them.'

'Did he tell you what I did that prompted him to disappear all of a sudden without explanation?'

'He kept saying, "She knows the reason."'

'But I don't know!'

'If you don't know the reason, God does. But, provided you were wronged, He intended this split as a blessing for you that you will appreciate later on.'

She said with tears in her eyes, 'There is nothing more painful than the one you love accusing you over the truest things you gave him. For you to be faithful, and him to suspect that you betrayed him. For you to keep your promises, and him to cast doubts on it.'

I said, 'Perhaps somewhere deep inside he knows you were true to him. But the voice of that "maggot" was louder than the voice of his heart. He said hurtful things about you and absolutely wanted me to pass them on. If you heard them you'd die of dejection.'

'I want to hear them.'

'There's no need for more pain.'

'Don't take pity on me. I want to know how he talks about me, the man I loved to death who now wants me to die.'

'It wasn't him talking. It was the language of that insect eating away at his heart. He's a decent, gallant man. If he wasn't like that, you wouldn't have loved him in the first place.'

'But I am more decent than him. I never mentioned his name except to his credit. Why do men do a woman down when they leave? Why do they chew up her reputation in company? Don't they have sisters? Don't they have daughters?

I said, her tears apparent, 'Don't cry. Someone who does damage to the woman he loved only damages himself and defaces what was beautiful in his past. His memory will never forgive him. Do you know a greater revenge than this: looking backwards and seeing only ruins? Don't outdo him in horror and destruction. Preserve him as something beautiful in your memory. Only remember the beautiful and exceptional things you shared. That fabled moment of love the first time you saw him. The first text message you received from him. The first time your phone rang and it was him on the line. The first time he kissed you and your legs turned to jelly. The first time he met you at the airport. The first time he sat opposite you in a restaurant. Contemplate the splendid things at the beginning and leave the horrific ending to him, as long as he chose it. Believe me when you overcome the pain he's caused and forgive his abuse, you will become more beautiful. Then you will be able to love anew with greater joy.'

'But I've never wanted to love anyone else.'

'In spite of that, from now on you will not be able to love a man who sent you a sack full of accusations and insults via me.'

It was unavoidable. Maybe she needed to hear his hurtfulness in order to be cured of it.

I opened the sack. I told her everything all in one go. I described to her the fragments of the bullets that I had taken in her place. She kept asking for all the details, for every word he had said, how many cigarettes he had smoked, the clothes he was wearing, the colour of his hair after her, the time he arrived and the time he left.

Then, as though she had taken a course of medicine in one go, in the space of a moment she became a different woman.

From a blow some are reborn and some die in our hearts.

I did not see her crying after this, nor did she bring him up. But to me she seemed more beautiful every time I met her.

> Human beings are not born once and for all on the
> day their mothers give birth to them, but life obliges
> them over and over again to give birth to themselves
> —Gabriel Garcia Marquez

Selected tales of stupid women

A MAN BELIEVES HE HAS ACHIEVED HIS END WHEN A WOMAN SUBMITS TO HIM. WHEREAS A WOMAN BELIEVES THAT SHE HAS ONLY ACHIEVED HER END WHEN SHE FEELS THAT A MAN HAS ESTEEMED WHAT SHE HAS GIVEN HIM

—Balzac

[illegible] wrong [illegible]

[illegible] India [illegible]

[illegible]

[illegible] in their [illegible]

[illegible] communities [illegible]

[illegible] you [illegible]

[illegible] believe [illegible]

Things will turn up at the wrong time
others as if they hadn't come
yet others arrive in haste
only to depart
before you understand that things have their moment

Things that weep for their owners
others that mock
lovers who weep for something
only ever found in their heads

Things that promise beautiful things
others that menace you
things that lie
things that lament
things that fleece you
others you don't believe
except at the end of everything

The Author, from 'Other Things', 2008

The first tale

Sigh no more, ladies, sigh no more,
Men were deceivers ever
—Shakespeare

She measured his love for her in the cigarettes he did not smoke. She would say, 'Every cigarette you do not light is a day you give me, to be added to the lifetime of our love.'

What high hopes she had of saving him from the clutches of nicotine. But on the day he quit smoking he stubbed out his last cigarette in the ashtray of her heart. He left her the ash of a woman, and gave his days to come to a woman who puffed on men.

The second tale

LOVE IS A SWEET TYRANNY, BECAUSE THE LOVER ENDURETH HIS TORMENTS WILLINGLY

—Proverb

If she saw an elegant man, she forgot to admire him. She just looked at his suit and imagined how good it would look on her lover.

When she spotted men's clothes in a shop window, they seemed to have been tailor-made for him. No other man had the right to wear them.

Her eyes would buy him everything beautiful she came across. Her heart would get him what her pocket couldn't. Whenever he took off something of hers, maybe he put *her* on again. When the coffers of his heart were full to the brim with her love, he pulled her off and donned another woman. He had become too elegant for 'rags of love'.

The third tale

WHEN A WOMAN GETS INVOLVED WITH A MAN,
SHE IS QUICKER TO BELIEVE THAN HIM.
IT WILL BE EASIER FOR HIM TO FOOL HER
THAN FOR HER TO FOOL HIM
—Abbas Mahmoud el-Aqqad

Whenever a new mobile phone hit the market, she would give it to him as a present so as to lengthen the life of his voice and have a portion of his breath. Her wish was to become the only avenue for his words, to share his touch with the phone, to ensure her place in his breast pocket, to be within reach of his heart and hand.

After the third phone, he said 'I divorce you' three times. He left her heart open to the elements and 'out of coverage'.

Without saying anything, without any explanations, he declared himself 'out of service'.

In fact, he had started working round-the-clock as servant to a woman allegedly called 'Betrayal'.

The fourth tale

BEAUTY IS IN THE EYE OF THE BEHOLDER
—Plato

For years she'd been telling him, 'You're so handsome!' She saw him with the eyes of the heart, the eyes of the past and of tomorrow, eyes thankful and grateful to life, the eyes of songs and poems, women's eyes, faithful eyes, stupid eyes.

All these eyes of hers were busy polishing his image. The day she fell in love with him she became all eyes.

She did not leave herself ears to ask why she never heard him say, 'You're so beautiful!', while the eyes of all those around her spoke this.

The space of her love was so vast, there was room for all his faults. His love was so narrow that not a stray unplucked hair on her face passed unnoticed.

Love to faults is always blind
—Shakespeare

The fifth tale

WOMEN ALWAYS WORRY ABOUT THE THINGS MEN FORGET
MEN ALWAYS WORRY ABOUT THE THINGS WOMEN REMEMBER
—the Author

Before him she hadn't been a woman; before her he hadn't been alive.

The day she met him, he had his back to life. Prior to her, he had only been a flirt with death, urging it on and killing time by zapping his days as though in a videogame.

She loved the lyricism of his depression, his hauteur, the innocence of his feelings, his loyalty, his memory, his belated childhood. She breathed life into him so he would live, as if she were his mother. She shared her breaths with him, she protected him with her fear, she guarded him with her prayers. She made him love beauty, the seasons, the rain, the sea, travel, poetry, openness, dancing. She made him love to love, love to be a man. She gave him the treasure of hope so he would forget the way to her rival in love: the grave.

One day he came to her in all his finery, happier than he had ever been. He was wearing the suit he had bought with her. He invited her out to celebrate his graduation from the academy of joy.

In the car he played the songs that they danced to together. She clung to him overjoyed. But he suddenly stopped the car and asked her to get out.

He left her trembling and in disbelief at the entrance to the cemetery and went to hold his wedding to life.

There are only two kinds of men – the dead and the deadly

—Helen Rowland

The sixth tale

MOST PRINCES ARE LIKE CHILDREN, OVERLY SPOILED,
BUT THEY ARE QUICK TO FORGET.
—Jean le Rond d'Alembert

All she asked from God was to send her a man to love and protect her, to give her his name and to whom she would give beautiful children. When a prince came into her life she couldn't believe the generosity of fate. His jet landed in her heart and he disembarked preceded by bouquets of roses, presents, and whisperings on the phone saying, 'You will be mine.'

Days of amorous vertigo. Then one day she opened her eyes to the roar of his jet. The dream had flown off to another woman, taking with it her dream of a white dress.

For years since she's remained in the airport watching the take-offs and landings. She doesn't expect his return, but she can no longer be satisfied unless love comes out of the skies in a private jet.

She could not forget that for a few days she was a princess, but for years she has forgotten how to live like a woman.

The seventh tale

THERE IS NO PERFECT LOVE, OR PERFECT CRIME
—Popular saying

He loved her, he pampered her, he desired her, he worried about her, he protected her, he cried for her, he made her cry. He was not jealous over her from other men, but jealous that she should not fail. He wanted her to be the best in every subject. He was harsh with her so that she did not accept less than the pinnacle of success. He polished her so that she shone like a diamond wherever she was. He put her on the top rung, then pulled the ladder out from under her so she wouldn't slip a fraction below his dreams.

He passed through her life like a river, heading for the sea without noticing the good he left behind on her banks.

He wanted her to be a big girl, as if he had fathered her. She did not realise he wished her like this to give birth to him.

This kind of paternal love, when it walked away, left behind the taste of eternal orphanhood.

To get over him she took to imitating him. She mothered the one she loved after him. She loved him, she pampered him, she worried about him, she protected him, she cried for him, she made him cry. She was not jealous over him from other women, but jealous that he should not fail. She wanted him to be a big boy, as if she had given birth to him.

This man disappointed her.

He did not realise that a woman who lavishes all these maternal feelings on a man wants him as a father!

Love repeats itself.

The eighth tale

WOMAN IS THE SHE-CAMEL THAT HELPS MAN TO CROSS THE DESERT
—Proverb

She loved him so much she converted to his faith and conformed to his memory. She changed her blond hair for Bedouin black, her sunglasses for Arab kohl and her summer resorts for the tents of his people. When she had no kin left but him and no family-tree, she planted a sapling in the forest of his tribe. She came to have kinship with every palm tree in his territory, with every camel in his desert, with every minaret in his country calling to prayer.

She would perfume her clothes before seeing him. She would burn incense at the entrance to any tent he lodged in and slaughter an animal out of joy at his visit. When she outshone him in 'bedouinity', he sent her a letter from his residence in London saying, 'I'm curing myself of old-fashioned love. I'm really sick. In my malady lies my medicine.'

Like a true Bedouin woman she resolved not to cry. She left him to the beds of the blonde and announced her marriage to the desert.

The ninth tale

A PAIR OF TRUE LOVERS ARE LIKE A PAIR OF LIPS. THEY MAY PART AT A WORD, BUT QUICKLY BECOME JOINED TOGETHER AGAIN
—Mohammed al-Sayyid Mohammed

One of the tribal-chiefs of love told me in the presence of his beloved, whom he had just got back together with, 'I can no longer bear to quarrel with her for more than a few days. Tell me how long you need to forgive someone their mistake, and I'll tell you how much you love them.'

For years my intimate friend had been blessed with the forgiveness of this unusual Bedouin. She finally invited me to meet him when he visited Beirut.

In my honour, or in the honour of forgetting, they held a dinner party where they would make me bear witness to their love; I had long been a witness to their disagreements and separation.

In fact, this sleek man in his forties was present to make pleadings in the only case that interested him: the captivating fidelity of a rare breed of men. My friend, unbeknown to me, had smuggled him a draft of this book. He said that I had done him an injustice in telling their story from her perspective. He agreed, however, to serve as an example for lovers, on the condition that I made it clear that my friend was the first love in his life, and that over the course of ten years of love's emotional highs and lows he had never loved anyone else and never cheated on her, despite his frequent travels and many opportunities. He bravely confessed that he had tried to sleep with another woman, during a long separation when her rejection had hurt him. But at the last moment he cancelled the planned fling and continued to hold aloft the banner of romantic defiance in loyalty to her.

He said, 'I went back with my tail between my legs when I wronged her. I like to rebel against my masculinity. Apologising means a return to childhood; cleansing the self of sins such as deceitfulness, pride, being controlling, selfishness and being mean. A woman feels that everything she does to preserve her dignity before her lover is to her credit. But, despite my pride, I see it to my credit to squander my dignity under the feet of the one I love.'

I was in the presence of a lover from the lords of loyalty. He had taken great strides in educating himself to be faithful to reach such a status.

A lover that love longs for and boasts of among men.

I asked him apologetically, 'If you like, I will delete those paragraphs where I presented you in a bad light.' He replied laughing, 'Don't do that. That fellow's also me!'

I understood why my friend, who under special circumstances had crossed paths with another man, had nevertheless not been able to forget him.

The heart forgets those who betray it. But it cannot forget loyalty.

The tenth tale

WE MUST GIVE MORE IN ORDER TO GET MORE. IT IS THE GENEROUS GIVING OF OURSELVES THAT PRODUCES THE GENEROUS HARVEST
—Oriso Swett Marden

Now this one I thought was the most foolish of women, except whenever I brought her to mind I did not find a category of lovers for her; as though she stood for love itself. I met her two years ago at Boston University. When I finished my lecture, she asked me a question that revealed her disappointment in men. She said, 'Why do the men in your novels remain faithful to the last page? Are you describing them as you knew them, or as you wished them to be? Your men don't exist except in books.'

I gave her an answer after the lecture, and we became friends for a few days. She hid her wound from me until the day I asked her to accompany me to a shop to buy a present for my husband.

She seemed keen to come along and was happy taking me to a shop she said she knew.

Inside the shop her glow dimmed. I saw her in a state of stunned silence walking around the departments and checking the prices of some suits. But when the assistant came to offer his help, she thanked him and continued looking round on her own. She hadn't come to buy, but to relive the moments of her purchasing a happiness that time had stripped away. Happiness reflected in an item of clothing on display with a dangling price tag that anyone who wished could buy.

Her tears defeated her. It was as though she'd taken me there to tell me what she hadn't said the first day.

She had loved him for years. As an émigré maybe he was looking for an Arab love, but he had found a stupid love.

She was a legal adviser. She supported his studies. She wanted him to be the biggest Arab lawyer in Boston. On trial days she would wake up before him. She would repeat in his earshot that the law was also a culture and that every case of his had to be an event. In ignorance of the greater event awaiting her, she changed his life and his interests, his appearance, the way he carried himself, his ignorance about women. How could she know that what he had learnt from her would entice him to browse the pages of other books. But she was content not to have him all to herself. She knew that she was sharing him in secrecy with an American wife.

Her love even overflowed to that woman, in gratitude for the years she had taken care of him when he first arrived as a young man from his country. She came to know her tastes and her favourite perfume. She would buy her presents for the holidays. The wife thought they were from her husband.

When she visited Syria on holiday, she came back with luxurious tablecloths and other presents for the house. The husband gave them to a wife unaware that the heart of a woman who loved her husband was adorning her house in secret and taking pleasure in welcoming guests along with her.

She woke up belatedly. Without her knowledge she had prepared him for a third woman. His excuses were ready and his actions premeditated.

The man whom she had wanted to bring back to his roots ripped the roots of any future love for an Arab out of her heart. She said, 'What's amazing is that I have managed to place him outside my life, my heart and my bed. But, when I pass by a shop where I used to buy him clothes, I still find myself going in and checking out the new season's line and looking for the colour that will suit him and his size. I wish I could buy him the most beautiful suits and choose matching shirts and ties. Whenever I find anything right for his daughter I break down in tears. How often I had put her before myself. I hoped I could prepare her wedding, walk her up the aisle and give her my jewellery. I was the Arab mother she didn't know existed. Even his wife, not a year passed without me being sad at seeing a gift pack of her favourite perfume on display for the holidays and not being able to give it to her as a present.'

I said in amazement, 'Surely, you're not being honest in what you're saying.'

She said, 'I swear it's true. My sadness isn't out of regret for what I gave him, but for what it's no longer in my power to give. Is there any greater misery than no longer being able to give to the one you love? It's the painful suppression of your natural instinct to be generous. Before the suits hanging in the shop, which I can afford but my heart cannot have, I cried. At that point I was sure he was dead to me.'

Someone dead is someone you can no longer give anything, but who can, even when they're gone, give you as much pain as they wish.

She picked up a leather jacket hanging on a rack and continued, 'Three years ago I gave him the exact same jacket with the lining to ward off the Boston chill. What really makes me happy today, even after love has died, is that this leather jacket will still protect him from the cold when he goes out of the house to meet another woman.'

Prior to this woman, I did not know that love is lavished not spent. It is gauged by the heart not the pocket. Thus separation impoverishes the generous lover until they end up living on the memory of giving and consoling themselves with this, as though giving was itself the reward of love. It takes them a long time to forget, when they're unable to give, because their suffering is greater than the pain inflicted upon them.

The tango of forgetting

THAT WAS TOMORROW BECAUSE I STILL LOVED YOU
THAT WAS YESTERDAY BECAUSE YOU HAD FORGOTTEN ME

—Ghada al-Samman

Forgetting, please give me your hand
So I can walk the cities of memory with you
Separation has ripened
On my lips have bloomed farewell kisses
I'm yours to pluck. Forgetting, plant a kiss on me

Forgetting, O my forgetting
A woman who resembled me once cried
Because of a man who so looked like you
Here she is today, consoled
He is there, she is here, dancing with you

My fate, my hope, my man above men
My forgetting
Dance with me, embrace me, make me fly, make love to me
Say, 'My, how beautiful you are.'
You I celebrate, to you I'm true
If you're always mine and I'm always yours
I'll never don mourning garb for love

The Author, from 'Forgetting, Plant a Kiss on Me', 2008

The tight-fitting shoes of new love

WE WEAR OUR HEARTS ON OUR FEET. SHOES ARE THE BEST INDICATOR OF THE STATES OF FEELING SOMEONE IS GOING THROUGH. SHOES ARE DECORATED WITH HOLES AND, SOMETIMES, WITH SCARS

—June Swann (shoe historian)

Love founds itself on a new memory. It needs a waiter to clear the table and shake out the tablecloth before it will sit down to eat.

We flee from savage memories to a new love which will savage us subsequently. But we want it anyway, in order to escape a previous love. We're exactly like someone escaping a fire in their house by jumping from the top floor. We're not worried about a few broken bones. What matters is not to burn to death, to save our skin from the flames. At that instant we pay no heed to what awaits us on the ground as we fling ourselves into the unknown.

When you take refuge in new love to forget a grand one, expect not to find a love that fits.

It will be painful and irritating like a pair of new shoes. You want it because it is elegant and perhaps expensive, because it matches your clothes. But it doesn't go with your heart and you won't be able to walk with it. You will convince yourself, for a long or short while, that if you persevere a bit you will be able to wear it. However 'the shoemaker wants us to feel pain so that we remember him'. You will pretend that the blisters left on your feet are superficial and can be treated with sticking plaster. All true, but in the main you won't be able to walk very far in these shoes. Your feet don't want them. They have got used to an old well-worn pair which they walked in for years. This is what the ancients meant by 'your past keeps you company', when with every step you take you cannot help taking your heart backwards.

If you're going out with a handsome, rich or important man, your friends may say, 'You're so lucky to have him!' Only your heart, which you slipped on like a shoe and is having trouble keeping abreast, is asking you to go home and take out your old pair of shoes from the box of the past.

When I tried to persuade Camellia to open her heart to a new love and accept talking to another man, even if only on the phone, she totally rejected the idea. She said, 'If my phone cheats on him, tomorrow my heart will and then my body. Aren't you the one who said that the death of a grand passion is more beautiful than the birth of a minor love?'

I was at a loss. 'Yes I did,' I said.

'What I want is for you to help me survive while this grand passion dies inside me. I don't want to miss one day, or one moment, of its magnificent demise. The lion has a majesty in death that the dog lacks in life. Even if it's dying, I wouldn't swap the body of this lion for the company of a stray dog!'

My problem with my friends is that they read my books. When they brandish my words in my face I have to admit defeat. I no longer knew a cure for Camellia. She wants to forget and doesn't want to; she wants to get better and doesn't want to; she wants her old shoes but knows that in the end, on the day she's certain that they are totally worn out and that no cobbler can fix them, she'll need a new pair. She cannot keep walking the pathways of life and the avenue of love barefoot.

Those whose life is miserable on account of the pain of new shoes or the memory of old shoes should give many thanks to God that they have feet, I mean a heart, to traverse the pathways of life. Some come and go without leaving the spot. Life has not given them a pair of 'loving' feet. Those, God has not blessed even with love's misery and agony.

> I complained I had no shoes until I met a man who had no feet
>
> —Confucius

The lovebird you weren't expecting

I WON'T WAIT LONG HERE, BUT IT WOULD BE LOVELY IF YOU CAME
—Abbas Beydoun

For two months I have persevered in calling her every day on the phone so that my efforts should not go to waste. I have learnt that with love, as with antibiotics, you have to complete the course right up to the last day and the last pill to avoid any emotional relapse. Nothing will be of any use once lovesickness strikes worse than before.

My friend was getting better all the time, but she needed a new love to restore her to life. She had heeded all my advice. She had become more beautiful, more focused on herself and more attentive to her interests. But no man had come into her life. Perhaps she was still guarding the cage door, having waited a year for the return of the lovebird that had flown.

One evening I called her to suggest she accompany me to a poetry reading by a major poet who was visiting Beirut. Not giving her the opportunity to refuse, I said, 'I'll come by to pick you up. Be ready. I mean be beautiful. From now on I'll be taking you to every cultural event.'

In the face of her lassitude and reluctance I said, 'Leave the cage. Your bird won't come back as long as your hopping from one foot to another says that you're still waiting for him. I forgot to teach you the most important lesson: it's only when you're no longer waiting for love that it comes back. Only when you're not stalking it will its fatal thunderbolt strike like the first time.

When she came down from her house, I nearly gasped upon seeing her. I shouted at her in fun, 'I must be mad to go into the auditorium with you. You look so beautiful today!' She kissed me and said, 'But you're more beautiful. I love you.'

Like the last time years ago, when I bumped into her at a cultural event, I saw the crowd welcome her and everyone come and say hello. But this time she had lost her voice. She was content to listen.

Then all of a sudden she was no longer following the conversation around her. Her gaze was frozen on a man of distinguished appearance making his entrance. Rather as though all the men had vanished and only this man was left.

I caught her amazement. The man had no sooner seen her than he was heading over. It was as though he had come on her account, despite his appearing stunned to see her.

He didn't shake her hand or kiss her cheek. He basically said nothing, but everything about him was embracing her.

I never saw a tougher and more confusing love scene. Even for her, the film director, the lightning bolt of the encounter went beyond her cinematic imagination. It was as though I had brought her along to meet him. Perhaps in gratitude to me she said when she was introducing us, 'My friend the author . . .'

She added the description author to my name as if to say I was the one who had partnered fate in writing this coincidence.

The man lifted his eyes to me in an effortlessly captivating glance. He extended his hand in greeting with a restrained happiness and only said, 'Pleased to meet you.'

He showed nothing that suggested he had read my books or knew who I was. Perhaps he had heard of me, or perhaps not. Maybe he had seen me in the papers one day, maybe he'd never seen me before.

His senses, just like his memory, were captivated by the woman I was with. I was happy that they became oblivious to my silent presence that withdrew in the presence of love.

I moved away to leave them alone with their longing. Then I saw him say goodbye to her and head for the auditorium. A man as dashing walking away as he was approaching.

We waited a little before going in. She insisted on not accompanying him in and so fuelling gossip. Obviously, she wasn't listening to a word of what was being said. She was looking for him with the eyes of her heart. Her knees were knocking slightly.

All she said was, 'You won't believe what's happening.'

When I repeatedly put the question to her, 'What's happening?', she kept silent, or perhaps did not hear me. Her heart was only listening to his heart beating somewhere in the hall.

In the car, after an interval of silence, I tried to lure her into letting something slip. I said, 'I think I remember that man you said hello to. I don't know where I've seen him before.'

She made a joke to evade the question, 'Perhaps you came across him in your books. Didn't you say, "The most beautiful love, we find while looking for something else."'

I didn't understand. Had she come across her beloved after despairing of waiting for him, and gone on the chance of meeting someone else? Or had she found someone else while looking for him? For certain, he was an old flame whose love had been rekindled from the ashes.

She wasn't ready to talk. Basically, she hadn't spoken to anyone but this man. As if she had used him to break the silence of her mourning. I let her live her amazement at him.

I said to her during our goodbyes, 'The day after tomorrow we're going to the premiere of a film.' She answered, 'Make excuses for me. You know I don't like events like that.'

I said in fun, 'I can understand that. An event once every four years is enough for you to get love back. Even so, I'm not going to let you return to your lazy ways. I'll call you tomorrow. Perhaps you will have changed your mind.'

The next day, I tried in vain to contact her at our morning time. Her line was busy, and I was also busy getting ready to travel. Two days later, I tried to call her again at nine o'clock in the morning. She told me she had got up early and was having breakfast on the balcony. She asked me if I'd like to come by for breakfast. I replied that I was about to travel and had no time.

'How long will you be gone?'

'Two weeks. But rest assured, I'll call you from Algeria at the usual time.'

'Are you sure? It's so expensive. Please don't call me.'

I commented as a joke, 'What have my expenses to do with you? I'll call you because I need to call someone at nine o'clock!'

We both laughed a lot.

She said, 'Okay then. Give a single ring at nine o'clock. That'll be enough for me.'

I said, 'You're right. In the end, love and happiness only require one ring.'

I kept my promise so as not to break my habit.

For two weeks, I let her phone ring once at nine o'clock Beirut time, eight o'clock Algiers time, seven o'clock London time!'

Madness all over again

YOU ARE ALL STRIVING – THOUGH YOU MAY NOT BE AWARE OF IT – TO STRUGGLE OUT OF THE GLOOM OF THE COMMONPLACE IN ORDER TO REACH THE SPLENDOURS OF LOVE'S FAIRYLAND

—Baroness Orczy

As soon as I returned to Beirut I resumed my telephone habit. I started my morning by calling Camellia at our appointed time. Perhaps I would learn her news. The phone in her house finally rang. It wasn't engaged this time, though it had been every time I tried to call from Algeria. But the real surprise was that a man's voice answered.

In shock, I apologised to him and redialled. But it was the same voice at the other end of the line.

In mild disbelief, I asked him, 'Can I speak to Camellia?'

The man replied, 'She's at the hairdresser.'

'Nine o'clock in the morning at the hairdresser?'

All of these surprises collectively were more than I could take in. How to explain to him that nine o'clock in the morning was 'my time' and that it was most unlike Camellia to leave the house so early?

Besides, who was this man? This was definitely the most important question. But what right did I have to ask him when he was at her house and answering the phone in her absence.

I said apologetically, 'I'm her friend. I've been trying to call her for days, but she's always engaged. I just wanted to make sure she was alright, nothing more.'

'She's good. She's just busy getting ready to travel. We're leaving in the afternoon, so she's a bit tied up.'

'You're leaving today!?'

My tone was like that of a jealous lover who's discovered he's being cuckolded.

I tried to lessen the impact of my question with another question. 'That's sudden. Where are you going?'

'To Greece.'

Amazed, I said, 'When did the two of you decide on the trip?'

'Yesterday, but really, ages ago.'

I didn't discuss what he was saying. I wanted to discuss it with her.

When had this man come into her life? Was he the man she had met that day at the auditorium? Could she possibly go on a trip with a man she'd only met a few days before? Such behaviour wasn't like her. Perhaps the other one had returned. Why didn't she tell me then? Maybe she was afraid that I would, on the basis of a year's torture, advise her against him. What if he was an old friend or former fling who had now found a chance to re-enter her life? Lots of men wished she were theirs and were envious of the one she had chosen and cherished. It was as if her pathological loyalty to him was an outspoken insult to their masculinity. Perhaps now they had come back to try their luck.

I would lure him to speak. He might say something that gave him away. Yet he said something that surprised me.

'I'll tell her that you called.' Then he added with a sly laugh, 'Aren't you that friend of hers that's inciting her to forget?'

His polite sarcasm made me speechless, and furious. How had she revealed such a secret, blurting it out to the first man who came along? Or to the one who'd come back after I spent two months convincing her to forget him. Oh the folly of women!

Disguising my embarrassment, I answered him, 'I was only helping her to get well again.'

'You mean get miserable again. Once she had forgotten everything, would she have been happier? Love exists to make you forget death. When you give up any part of your memories, along comes death and occupies it.'

All the roles were reversed. I assumed the role of the accused, and I found myself on the defensive. 'I did not want her to get rid of her memories. No, just a man who tormented her, made her cry, made her miserable and forgot her.'

'Who says he forgot? Do you think only elephants remember? Only crocodiles cry? Only eagles are loyal?

Had this man come back after a year of absence to settle scores with me? Oh you foolish woman. It's as though she had spent the time I was gone telling him my recipes for forgetting!

To lighten the mood, I asked him playfully, 'Excuse me, are you an eagle?'

He gave an evasive answer. 'I wish I was an eagle! But I'm just a man. Though women generally don't differentiate between eagles and vultures. The eagle doesn't pick on carcasses and only comes back to his mate.'

'Why does he desert her then? Is it the call of the wild? Because his wings are too massive to keep him on the ground?'

'No. The tragedy of the eagle is that he is a lion with wings, the lion of the skies. But his mate only sees a bird. What do women know of the jealousy and pride of the lion? Of his madness when he doubts his mate and returns to teach her cubs a lesson.'

'As far as I know, he does that when he wants her, and she says no!'

'Nice. It looks as though you know more about animals than you do about men!'

'My facts are limited to those animals I've loved.'

'Next time, love an eagle so that you can be sure of his return. Elephants have vengeful memories.'

'That's the reason they die alone.'

'Did you love an elephant too?'

'I would have done, hungry for loyalty. But his faults outweigh his good points, so I ditched the plan. I'll make do with loving a man.'

'Why do women think all men are cheats? There are lords of loyalty ready to die for love. Just as there are women who cheat and strangle a man's desire to be loyal. A man dreams of a woman he can be true to. He can wait for her a year or longer. He'll turn to her memory to fend off all the women in the world just for the sake of that gasp of recognition when he comes back to her.

I suspected I had proof that he was the former lover. I asked him, 'Should I understand that you've returned from the past?'

He gave a cunning laugh and said, 'The past? No. I'm the man of the present.'

'Why are you defending the past then?'

'I'm not defending the past. I believe in the numerous lives of the one heart, nothing more.'

I was at a loss. This man was outside emotional space-time. I would never know who he was, but I expect he had loved her madly at some point in time.

He then said, 'Do you think lovers who have separated too soon are engrossed in forgetting? When it's not possible for you to love more, love less. Whenever love takes a step back, it rebounds stronger. It is nourished by its loss.'

He went quiet for a moment then continued. 'All the torment comes from you not knowing how the other is surviving the loss. And to whom they've turned to forget you.'

I wonder if he meant my friend? I was preparing my defence of her and I knew her as well as he did, if not better. I had been her friend for fifteen years; if this was a man she had loved in the past, she had been absolutely faithful to him. But love is never satiated or satisfied. It is the devouring and savaging of the other. Each of the two lovers think that what he or she has received is less than what he or she has given; that they have not totally and completely ravished their beloved. Something of one has been saved from the jaws of the other, and over this little something they fall out, and split up!

Before I started my defence, his mobile rang and he was obliged, apologetically, to stop talking to me. Perhaps it was Camellia on the line. No doubt, she was not content with the messages she had sent him while under the hairdryer and now needed to hear his voice.

This call saved me a lot of arguing and the trouble of uselessly defending her. Besides, I would never know which one of them was right. The Lebanese proverb says, 'He who plays the judge between children condemns himself'. What about the one who plays judge between lovers then?

When his voice was gone I cursed him in my heart.

This man had messed with my head. Before talking to him I had been happy. I belonged to the Party of Forgetting but had become a Partisan of the Eagles. Had the conversation with him continued, I would have split from the Women's Party and joined the Men's Party,

I corrected myself: I would have joined the Lovers' Party. This man had trapped me with his words because he was pleading the defence for love. We are all of us weak before love. How could I declare war on a man who said he wanted to love a woman at every minute, and whose complaint against her was that she had kept some minutes for herself?

Do we want anything other than this man? Except this creature wasn't a man. He himself said he was an eagle, a lion. How would we live with him in a jungle where he is king? Why then have we women struggled for centuries?

In fact, we have struggled to restore our rights from this kind of man in particular. Then we struggled once again to restore him in particular. We still don't know what specifically we want from him.

I personally do not know what I want from him. I feel that I was still hungry to talk with him. There are things I could have got him to divulge while he was still jubilant at the return of love. This would be the ideal moment to bag his confession. A time would come later when the man's chatter would cease. Then, you would need to seat him in the electric chair to extract a word.

I decided to call him back. I had a logical pretext.

'Hello.'

'Hi.'

'I'm sorry. I know you're getting ready to travel. Thanks for giving me some of your time.'

'When I give, I forget.'

'But I am obliged not to forget your kindness, despite my working on forgetting!'

'Is that why you bought a website for forgetting?'

Good God, she even told him that!

I said defiantly, 'No, I bought two. I even got nessyane.net*!'

'It's a bad investment. You've bought your bankruptcy. There's nothing poorer than having no memories!'

'I won't be the only one bankrupt. The whole world is going through an economic crisis. Everyone's bankrupt.'

'And because they're bankrupt they need their memories and their past.'

'Their beautiful memories yes, not the terrible ones. What's required is a selective memory. We can't allow those who've hurt us to continue to mess up our present. Being hurt once is enough. And don't say, "Forgive!" I'm not going to forgive. Are you?'

'You mean in love? Love is essentially pain. Because you don't take it in limited doses. You consume great quantities of the beloved and get addicted to him. You're hurt by him and hurt him because of your ever increasing need for him. Then you rebel and forsake him.

* The author's official website is nessyane.com.

You both make each other ill. I would only forgive in one case: when the one who hurts you out of love is more tortured than you.'

'Thanks. It's as though you were giving me good news.'

'No, I'm giving you experience.'

'Are you a veteran of love?'

'A veteran of hurting!'

I tried to understand 'hurting' in its finer sense.

I said, 'In all cases, it would be a pleasure to be a witness to this love.'

As if to remind me of my previous role in persuading her to forget him, and to end my involvement in their story, he said, 'Lovers and the honourable have no need of witnesses.'

It was clear he was admonishing me and nullifying my role in their life from now on. Like all men he had no faith in his lover's circle of friends. He was aware of their ability to form a bloc and confront him at the first disagreement. Like any ruler, he would not consent to a coalition forming outside his party.

I had the feeling that he might make her happy for a few days then be left alone to torment her. She would not have the courage to come back and complain about him to me again.

I said, 'I called you back because I've got a request for you. Perhaps you won't hear from me again. Perhaps we'll never meet. But I have faith in your decency. Whoever you are, promise me not to make her suffer. She has suffered enough over the last few months. I no longer have the time or energy to support her once more. You be her support, even when you're her opponent. I entrust her to your keeping.'

He was silent then said, 'The precious are the trust of the precious,' and hung up.

The language of this man has not left me.

From 'Hello' to all the questions he left behind.

The joy of getting back together with . . . his ordeals

ONE CANNOT LOVE AND BE WISE
—Proverb

Love returned.

Camellia went back to her old habit.

Her rapacious passion ravaged my nerves, and I expect it will ravage her dreams once again.

Such feelings were too powerful to stay on course. She was draining her friends with the coming and going of the tide. This was passion, the epitome of extremism. But shortly Camellia would weep at his tyranny, his injustice and his rejection. And after today, I wouldn't be there as a shoulder for her to cry on.

For two months I fought to the death in defence of forgetting. For her sake and for the sake of other idiots like her. I bought up the world's stock of forgetting and set up a website. I founded a party and appointed myself as general-secretary and deputy. Confident that if I stood as a candidate in the Lebanese elections (which is my right being also a Lebanese citizen) I would sweep the board. I would not leave a seat for the grandees of the 8th of March or the 14th of March alliances. I wouldn't need drums or fifes, liras or dollars, to convince five of every six voters to chose me, given that this is the ratio of young women to each and every big man in Lebanon!

I provide this clarification so that none of you should say, if I win by a margin that goes beyond the bounds of logic, that I rigged the elections.

In all cases, it's not likely that my sense of pride will allow me less than a crushing victory over all those persuaded to run against me. To 'crush' is a time-honoured right of our Arab democracy.

Despite electoral campaigns in Lebanon costing more than anywhere else on earth, I will not require financial support from any regional power. I do not want my election campaign to be adopted by the construction mafia or big-time crooks on my promise of deals and posts to milk. Nor will I make a grab for the bread of the poor to fund giant wall-posters and campaign leaflets out of state coffers.

Thank God forgetting is a mass demand when it comes to women. It does not need promoting or pillorying.

The election results will qualify me to declare myself president of the Republic of Forgetting for all women of the Arab world. At this point I will for once act like a man. May the sisters in struggle forgive me, but I will not consent to share or rotate power with anyone. Just as our rulers distract their peoples with wars and fateful issues, I will distract women with shopping and make it their number one issue. I will for their sake instigate national holidays for shopping and seasons for the sales that start in January and run to December, so that I can be free to rule and guard the throne of government.

There is prestige in being the guardian of the throne, even if it's a seat vacant for forgetting.

I will undoubtedly be confronted with the problem of succession, given that the office demands a woman and I only have sons.

I have however, thanks be to God, found a solution that conforms to the Arab fixes for the inheritance of power. I hope you understand my delaying the publication of this plan until my forthcoming book.

The real problem will be ruling the millions of idiotic women who do not follow the party line, and do not know exactly what they want from life. They are members of the Party of Forgetting, but they are eyeing up men. They say no, but they mean yes.

Like this loon whom I spent two months convincing to forget. No sooner had this man said 'Hi' than she said 'Bye' to me and went over to him. Indeed, she didn't even say 'Bye' to me, and didn't tell me what had happened. Nor how matters had developed so quickly between them and the miracle occurred. Is it not my right to know? I call her and up pops a man. Until now I still don't know who he is. Seriously: he knows everything about me, and I don't even know his name.

God, happiness is so selfish. And love so indifferent. When love comes along with its fabled happiness, sister forgets sister, girlfriend forgets girlfriend, the father becomes unknown to his children, and children to their mothers.

Love inhabits a galaxy off the astronomers' charts. Camellia is now on a planet light-years away from my terrestrial abode. She can't even see me with the naked eye. In short, I no longer exist for her, but for two months I was her whole life.

I picked up the phone and called her on her mobile. She answered with a gasp of delight from her planet amidst the clamour of the hairdresser's.

'Hi my darling, I missed you. When did you get back? Let me know you're okay.'

'I got back yesterday. I tried to call you, but . . .'

'I can't hear properly. I'm at the hairdresser's.'

'When can I see you?'

'It'll be difficult to meet today. I'm leaving for the airport in two hours. I'll see you when I get back next week or call you from there.'

'I need to see you before you leave.'

'Is there something wrong?'

(Heavens above, she's asking *me* if there's something wrong or some 'latest news'.)

'There are lots of things. We have to meet before you leave. Give me the address of the salon and I'll be with you in half an hour at most.'

I wrote down the address on a blank sheet of paper on my desk. Then a thought occurred to me. I sat down at my desk, turned over the piece of paper and drafted the words of a pledge. Talk in such situations would be useless.

I hurriedly got dressed and caught up with her at the hairdresser's. The dye was still on her hair. Slightly puzzled, she stood up to greet me.

'You've had me worried. Is there something wrong?'

'I wanted to catch you my dear so that you could sign this piece of paper for me before you catch your plane.'

She looked at the paper in amazement, took it from me and began to look it over with curiosity.

The nail polish on her fingers was still wet, and she picked the sheet up gingerly between two fingers. She was dumbfounded and didn't grasp the subject.

I took the paper from her and put it on the small table in front of her under the mirror. I said, 'I called you at home, and a man answered. I expect he's your awaited lover-boy, or an ex-lover, it doesn't matter.'

She seemed confused. I said, 'You shouldn't have hidden the news from me. As if I thought you'd be afraid of my reaction. I'm not against him coming back. Or against a new man entering your life. Forgetting isn't an end, it's a means leading to another love. All I wanted was for you not to be tortured anymore because of a man. Nothing warrants the pain you lived. Don't allow a man to amuse himself by tormenting you for no reason, and then come back when he wants as though nothing had happened.'

She responded, 'He was also tortured.'

'He was the one who wanted that. That's his business. I hope you won't cover the costs of his suffering and apologise to him. Men love role reversal.'

She wasn't very interested in what I was saying. She asked me excitedly, 'Since you've spoken to him, how did you find him?'

'Really, I'm happy that life has rewarded you with this man. I don't know if he's the one you were waiting for. I think he deserves it. That man is of the breed of eagles. I've dubbed him "the eagle-man". He's an unusual man in our times. My fear was that you had been waiting for one of those dickey-birds who peck at crumbs wherever they are and fly off.'

She was happy with what I said. Her features glowed with joy as though she had passed an exam.

I said, 'Still, you ought to know that men like him will fly off again. Someone who was absent all that time has acquired immunity to loss. His wings are too big to be clipped, and his passion is too fierce not to hurt you again. Next time, your relapse will be worse and your pain greater, because I won't be around to support you.

She was silent and her colour suddenly blanched. But the voice of her heart was louder than my voice. She believed half of what I said, putting all her money on the miracle. Perhaps he did come back for comfort and to comfort her. He was no fledgling this eagle.

I said, 'I expect that what I said to you over those two months has evaporated in your joy at his return. Just retain at least four pieces of the advice I gave you. If you memorise them and put them into practice no man will make you suffer from now on. I wrote them down for you on the piece of paper in the form of a pledge. I want you to read it carefully and sign it at the bottom.

She laughed and said, 'Are you serious? Have you gone mad?'

'No. But I know that happiness has stripped you of your good sense.

'The law of love does not protect the stupid or the reckless. I want you, now, before you join up with him, to read this page and memorise it like you did your lessons at school. These bits of advice will save you a great deal of pain in future.'

She cast a quick glance over what was in it, then said disdainfully, 'I know this. You told me before.'

'It's not important that you know them, but that you remember them. Besides, I want your signature at the bottom of the page.'

She took a pen out of her purse and, laughing, signed at the bottom, 'Camellia'.

I said, 'I want your name in full, with your father's name and your surname. That's how a woman signs who takes herself and her pledges seriously.

She said laughing, 'Are you serious? You want my family tree?'

'Of course. A woman signs with her roots, not her name, so that her roots keep her grounded. Plus you should learn to place your father's name between you and any man. Don't enter love cut off from the tree and your beloved become the last stroke of the axe.'

I don't know whether my words convinced her or whether she was in a hurry to get my sermon over with. She wrote her full name on the paper. During this the hairdresser appeared and took her to wash the dye out of her hair.

I said while taking the paper from her and kissing her goodbye, 'I'll keep it to remind you of its injunctions in case you come back to complain to me about your disappointments. Enjoy your trip, you really deserve it.'

On the way home I mocked myself.

Here am I alone. In my handbag a contract with forgetting: in her handbag a ticket to the archipelago of love.

How absurd!

The charter of feminine honour

I the undersigned state that I have read these injunctions and solemnly promise before myself and before love and before the readers and before all God's creation, the amorous and the penitent, from now until doomsday to adhere to the following:

* To enter love totally certain that there is no such thing as eternal love
* To acquire immunity to shocks and expect anything from the beloved
* Not to cry on account of a man, for no man deserves my tears. Those truly deserving of them would not bear to make me cry.
* To be ready to forget, as men forget.

Signed: Camellia Fouad al-Hashim

Beirut
9 a.m.
18 April 2009

Note: each reader is requested to add her signature to the bottom of this page and at www.nessyane.com.

Now leave me alone!

I HOLD A DEGREE FROM THE UNIVERSITY OF FORGETTING BUT MY HANDS ARE EMPTY LIKE A SHIRT HANGING ON THE LINE
—Swedish poet Tomas Tranströmer

The next day I woke up early. My friend whom I had tried to save from the nine o'clock memory had departed and bequeathed me her 'time'.

Off she went with her lover and left me the corpse of a telephone to stand in for her. 'If you throw the drowning man a life-ring, he's definitely going to ask to come on board.'

Camellia had embarked once again on the ship of love. Perhaps she had reached some shore (I won't say dry land for I'm not certain what awaits her in the enchanted isles of love).

She had no sense left to remember me. I wanted her to forget him and she forgot me in her wake rowing in the sea of memory every day at the exact hour.

My voice had been an emotional trick to break her internal clock. To assuage with words the black-and-blueness of the bruises left by loss. Pills of compassion for her to take every morning to make her forget a telephone call that didn't come.

Damn her. She's hooked me on a telephone habit, and I now need rehab.

There are two options: to undertake a search for one of my girlfriends to call me at nine o'clock – and in this medicine is a malaise

I don't want to propagate – or to allow a man to perform this telephone mercy mission. Then I will have to turn to another man to rid myself of the tyranny of this habit and restore my freedom. That is repeat the folly of the Arab peoples who throughout history have gotten used to relying on an occupier to rid them of a despot.

There is another solution which has just occurred to me: to read every morning some pages of this book in the chance that I will learn from them how to forget. I know of no one for whom it would do more good than me.

I need to forget, in the first place, my friend and her lover, then the eagles among men, and the vultures, and all males, sparrows, lions and elephants, all the human beasts roaming this Earth: vipers, scorpions, chameleons, frogs and rabbits. 'What's the big deal with the animals?' Red Riding Hood and all the naive women who disagree with the commandments of forgetting will ask. They will be consumed by their lover the wolf, and I will not respond.

'Never explain yourself. Your friends don't need it and your enemies won't believe it.'

For your sakes I did what your dear grandmother – to whom you were taking a basket of fruit when the wolf harassed you in the forest – did not do. (Or whom you used as a pretext to go and harass the wolf.) I opened a 'romance rehab' for you on the Internet to receive the victims of wretched memories, with the intention of making you ready to face life once more.

Now, 'leave me alone'!

It's nine o'clock in the morning.

Here end Scheherazade's permitted words about your lives endured in the name of love. I've left you a blank page. Fill it up with whatever tales of yours you wish on love and forgetting.

Perhaps afterwards you will give the book to a lovesick friend, or to an ex-lover. Or, in your feminine wiles, you go as far as giving a copy to someone whom you think clinched the deal by taking your place in his life. Perhaps she will benefit from this book, if she hasn't read it – and I expect she hasn't!

I was busy putting together the manuscript of this book to review before sending it to press when the phone rang.

It startled me. Seriously? I didn't believe it. At nine o'clock in the morning precisely the phone rings! It certainly wasn't Camellia. Who could it be then, with this unknown number from far away?

It continued ringing with the insistence of new love in all its initial fervour and longing.

The phone wasn't ringing it was throbbing. The things around me started to dance and the papers on my desk to fly in delight. My wardrobe was urging me to be quick and answer. But suddenly I decided not to.

Writing about the 'Season of Separation' would not be possible with a phone that throbs.

'I hope you will take my sacrifices into consideration!'

Don't forget in the open waters of forgetting, to sign in your turn the charter and send an acknowledgement of this to the nessyane.com website. To add to Camellia's signature and those of the party of friends and the masses of freedom fighters.

In theory, we should collect the signatures of 40,000 women, which is the print run of the first edition of this book (unless men buy up half the quantity out of curiosity or to usurp our right to forget.)

The most important thing is that you stick closely to the commandments of this pledge, thereby saving months of suffering and years of delusion.

I swear by Almighty God, by God, by God, if you do not learn your lessons, that I will write a book dedicated to men which you are banned from buying and where I will give them advice to forget you.

Get it into your heads, I no longer have any connection with forgetting. I'm off to work on 'The Book of Separation'.

I promise you it will be as beautiful as this book was useful.

I hope that none of you will come along in the future to complain to me of some amorous memory. From now own the Art of Forgetting is yours.

Abbas Beydoun (1945)	Lebanese writer and poet
Abbas Mahmoud el-Aqqad (1889–1964)	Egyptian journalist and poet
Abu Nawwas (756–814)	classical Arab poet
Ahmed Shawqi (1869–1932)	Egyptian poet
Bassam Hajjar (1955–2009)	Lebanese poet
Constantine P. Cavafy (1863–1933)	Greek poet
Einaya Jabir	Lebanese journalist and poet
Fairuz (1935)	Lebanese singer
Faisal al-Rashid	contemporary Kuwaiti singer
Ghada al-Samman (1942)	Syrian poet and novelist
Ghazi al-Quseibi (1940–2010)	Saudi Arabian politician and novelist
Hala Mohammed	contemporary Syrian poet
Ibn Zaydun (1003–1071)	poet from Islamic Spain
Ibrahim al-Koni (1948)	Libyan novelist
Ibrahim Nagy (1898–1953)	Egyptian poet
Kamil el-Shinnawi (1921)	Egyptian poet
Lubna	beloved of Qais in seventh century Arabic romance
Mahmoud Darwish (1941–2008)	Palestinian poet
Malik Haddad (1927–1978)	Algerian poet and Francophone writer
Muslim ibn Yassar	contemporary of Yaqub al-Hadhrami
Nizar Qabbani (1923–1998)	former diplomat and poet from Syria
Nour el-Sherif (1946)	Egyptian screen and TV actor

Qais	lover of Lubna in seventh century Arabic romance
Shahrazaad	pseudonym of contemporary Emirati writer and poet
Suheil Idris (1925–2008)	Lebanese journalist and writer
Talal al-Rasheed (1962–2003)	Saudi Arabian poet
Talal Salman (1938)	Lebanese journalist
Umm Kalthoum (1898–1975)	Egyptian singer
Unsi al-Hajj (1937)	Lebanese poet and critic
Wallada bint al-Mustakfi	poet. Daughter of Cordoban (1001–1080) Caliph Muhammed III.
Yaqoub al-Hadhrami	ninth-century Quran reciter

A Note On The Translator

Raphael Cohen is the translator of the novel *So You May See by Mona Prince* (AUC Press, 2011). He studied Arabic at Oxford and the University of Chicago and currently lives and works in Cairo.